A Desperate Way

A Desperate Way

Jim Gerlock

ISBN: 1546577750
ISBN 13: 9781546577751

Contents

Book cover is a picture of the concrete Dixie Highway in Central Georgia 1927 which was later named U.S. 41.

Prologue

On the enclosed Georgia map follow the dotted line on 41 Hwy. going south from Jonesboro to Haynesville. This Hwy was once the main artery carrying life's blood to many small towns along its route.

Now follow I-75 south and notice how it bypasses and isolates the small towns along 41 Hwy. This caused many a small town to suffer a severe economic depression.

This history is the back-drop for this novel which depicts what one of these towns did in a desperate way to survive. The towns, events, places, things and people in this novel are not real and only exist in my imagination.

Georgia Map

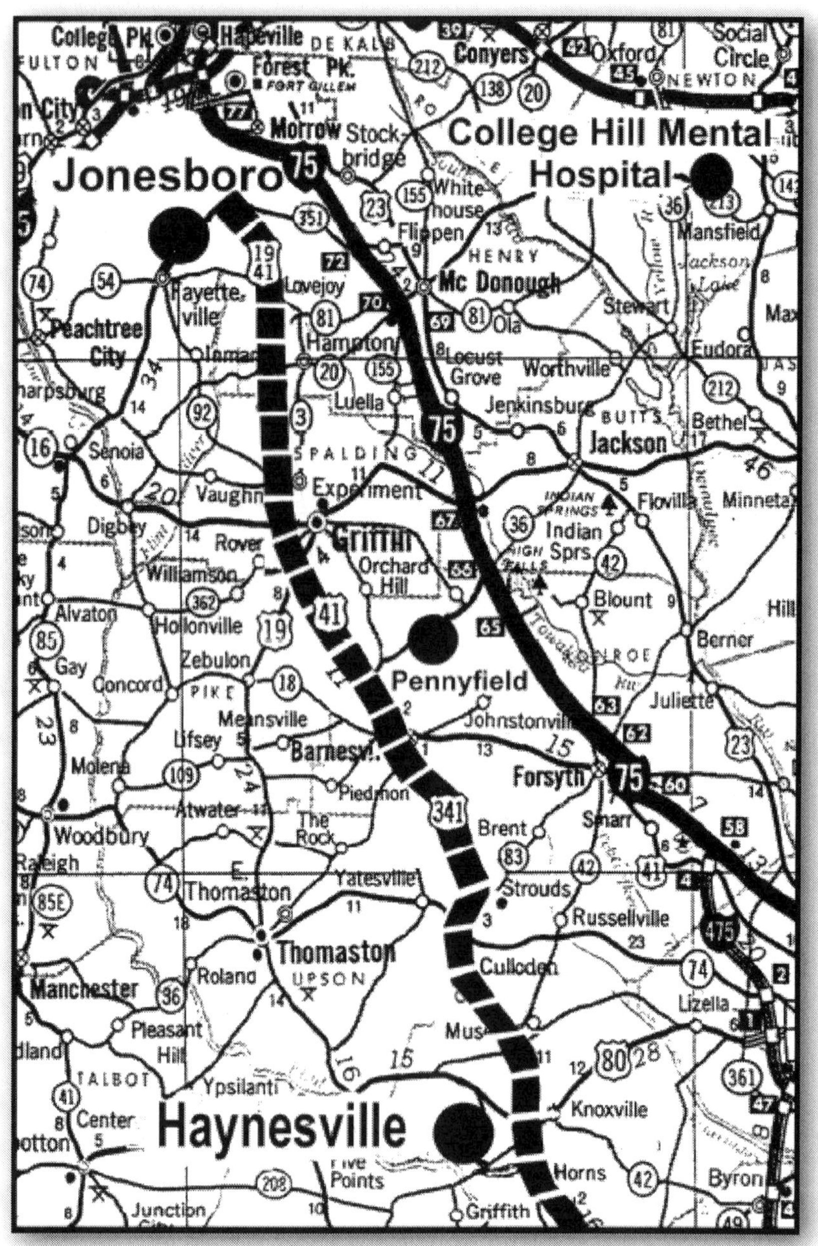

College Hill Mental Hospital
Jonesboro
Pennyfield
Haynesville
College PK.
Hapeville
Forest PK.
Morrow
Stockbridge
Conyers
Oxford
Social Circle
Whitehouse
Flippen
Mc Donough
Mansfield
Lovejoy
Fayetteville
Peachtree City
Hampton
Locust Grove
Worthville
Stewart
Eudora
Luella
Jenkinsburg
Bethel
Senoia
Jackson
Experiment
Vaughn
Flovilla
Digby
Griffin
Indian Sprs.
Rover
Orchard Hill
Williamson
Blount
Alvaton
Hollonville
Berner
Gay
Zebulon
Concord
Juliette
Meansville
Johnstonville
Lifsey
Barnesville
Molena
Forsyth
Piedmont
Atwater
Woodbury
The Rock
Brent
Smarr
Raleigh
Yatesville
Thomaston
Strouds
Russellville
Manchester
Roland
Culloden
Lizella
Pleasant Hill
Ypsilanti
Knoxville
Center
Horns
Byron
Five Points
Junction City
Griffith

Acknowledgements

With many thanks to my Julie and our special friend Kathy Abram

Chapter 1

The Trip Begins

Three weeks have passed since I had seen Vivian's burning body writhing on the floor like a snake spitting black smoke in all directions at The Haynesville Baptist Church. It's a scene I'll carry to my grave. And who knows? There I may see her again.

But today is a cold November morning and my wife Puddin and I are taking a trip from Jonesboro to her hometown Haynesville. Like an unwanted visitor frost has come overnight and lingers in the late morning sun. Puddin sits in our car waiting impatiently for me to load our suitcase into the trunk. Her chubby knees jitter like she's bouncing down a washboard country road. Our eyes meet as I pass by the car's window. Hers is an icy stare befitting the chilly winter's air. Rolling down the window she shouts,

"LET'S GET GOING! You know I wanna get to Haynesville before dark. Wanna meet with Judge Stoneridge about Mama's Will. Wanna see her grave too."

We've been married for twelve years and have been making this trip yearly to be with her parents for Thanksgiving and Christmas

Holidays. But today's trip is different. Both her parents are dead. And time has changed Haynesville so that it will never be the same again

Haynesville, Georgia has always been a small one stoplight peach orchard farm town with roots dating back to the Civil War. Iron crosses still mark Confederate Soldiers' graves in the cemetery behind The Haynesville Baptist Church. Sidewalks built above the street level so people would not get splattered with mud from horses' hoofs are reminders of the old horse and buggy days. Brick store fronts line the short streets.

I hate going there because it stirs the memory that'll haunt me forever. THE FIRE ! I had over slept the morning of the fire and arrived late at The Haynesville Baptist Church. The service was almost over so I decided to go down stairs to the kitchen for coffee. That's when I heard voices coming from behind the kitchen door.

"We gotta burn it down THIS MORNING!" a woman shouted. It was Puddin's mother shouting at Sheriff Tate.

"NO!" he answered.

"YOU GOTTA DO IT NOW!" She commanded in a high pitched hysterical voice.

"I CAN'T! MY DADDY'S UP THERE!," he answered. His voice, strong at first, soon faded into that of a beaten man.

"Burning up your daddy is perfect. They'll never suspected you did it. It'll be a perfect accident."

Suddenly their voices faded until all I heard was Rev. Boswell's blustering voice coming from the pulpit upstairs. I pressed my ear hard against the door to hear them more clearly when it sprang open causing me to lunge head first into the kitchen. I'll never forget the wild look in Vivian's eyes when she saw me. I startled her so she dropped the glass jug she was holding. It burst into pieces on the floor splattering gasoline all over her and the kitchen stove's open gas flame. In a flash, fire roared from the stove to the floor creating an inferno filled with burning, sizzling flesh. Her burning body writhed on the floor like a huge snake spewing oily black smoke in all directions. The smoke must have suffocated her for she died without making a sound. I tried to hide the horror by clenching my fists over my eyes when WHAM! Sheriff Tate yanked me out of the kitchen by my shirt.

"GO WARN THE OTHERS!" he shouted. **"GET THEM OUT BEFORE THEY'RE ALL BURNED ALIVE!"**

Panicked I scrambled up the steps to the church's sanctuary. Glancing back over my shoulder I remember seeing Sheriff Tate frantically trying to snuff out the flames from her burning body with his coat.

The Haynesville Baptist Church burned to the ground that sunday morning taking with it memories of funerals and weddings that had taken place there over the years. Puddin's mother was the only one to die in the fire. Her death was officially reported an accident to the Charity Life Insurance Co.

"My God. What are you doing?" Puddin shouts out the car window, "put the damn suitcase in the car and LETS GET GOING!" Her high pitch voice bellowing at me is a welcome sound for it brings me back to the present and away from that horrible sight. Suitcase loaded,

I slam the trunk lid shut so hard the car rocks up and down. Why am I taking my frustrations out on this car when it's Puddin who's killing me? The car chokes and sputters reluctant to leave the warmth of the garage and go out into the cold morning air. Slowly, I back the car out of the garage and drive down our cobbled stone driveway towards Old Jonesboro Road. The driveway is lined with leafless oaks. Their limbs decorated in white lace by the morning frost.

"Check the mailbox," commands Puddin. "I know Flavel's not gonna pick up our mail while we're gone. Can't depend on that fool to do anything right."

I check the mailbox and find a letter in it addressed to me. "Give it here," she says snatching the letter out of my hand and stuffing it under her seat. "I'll open it later."

We leave our English Tudor home behind and cross over the Morning Glory Creek Bridge and pass through the fog rising off its waters. Two miles pass and then a third. Our trip south from Jonesboro to Haynesville has begun.

"Why are you always upset with Flavel?" I ask.

"He does his best to look after our house every time we go to Haynesville." My question heats her anger to a boiling point and her icy stare turns into a scalding scowl.

"Don't talk to me about him. If you hadn't carried on so about him grieving over his wife's death, I'd never spoken to him again.. And don't go telling me how much you loved riding his school bus. Lord knows I've heard enough about that."

Puddin's right. Flavel had driven the school bus when I was a kid. Some of my happiest memories come from those **magical times.**

Flavel's bus was filled with bologna smells oozing from brown paper lunch bags and the spicy aroma from the boy's oil slicked hair. Up front sat the Busby brothers their breaths reeking with a salty smell from a breakfast of fat back bacon. Being poor, they wore the same clothes every day. In back, sat Claudia pleasing as a painting. A fresh ribbon adorned her hair each morning. It was gone by noon. We'd ridden Flavel's bus through all the seasons and felt *Fall's* cool winds sooth a *Summer's* hot sting and watched the leaves on the trees thick from a full Summer's growth turn into towers of gold and yellow hues in *Fall.* The leaves would fall to the ground withered and died at Thanksgiving. We rejoiced at Christmas when the front yards sprang forth reindeers, candy canes, and Santa Clauses. Some Santa Clauses were life size and stood in front yards while others rocked comically in chairs on front porches. Happy New Year and it was back to school again. The New Year brought a *Winter* freeze killing the grass and shrubs. Trees with their naked limbs silhouetted against a gray sky stood shameless along the roadside. *Spring* brought us new shoes and honey suckle vines climbing pasture fences and wild flowers dotting the fields. I thought this time would last forever. But like Flavel's school bus, my childhood days are gone. Now, I'm a prisoner chained in a rolling prison cell sentenced to drive Puddin into hell . . . her precious hometown Haynesville.

"Let's go the old way on 41 Hwy," I say timidly as we continue along Old Jonesboro Road going south toward 41 Hwy. "It's more scenic than I-75."

I always liked 41 Hwy with its 1940's-1950's history. People, with business sense, had seen a chance to make money from folks they called snowbirds migrating north from Florida's summer heat and south to Florida's warmth in winter along 41 Hwy. They built motels, restaurants, gas stations which provided a booming economy for the small towns along 41Hwy. Unfortunately, these towns began to wither and die after I-75 was completed in 1977.

My request to go on 41 Hwy is met with a "HELL NO!" from Puddin. Her wrath falls on me like a ton of bricks. "41's too slow. Stop and go, stop and go. We'll be inch worming our way to Haynesville all day."

She's right. Even with such nostalgic memories as Burma Shave Serial Signs: [Don't Take a Curve] --- [At 60 mph] ---

[We Hate To Lose] --- [A Customer], 41 Hwy could never compete with I-75's four lanes and speeds of seventy miles per hour.

Since we're not going on 41Hwy, we continue on Old Jonesboro Road crossing over the railroad tracks where us kids loved to watch the trains go by. A sight I'll never forget. It began with a kid, summoned by an air horn blast, poking his head out his daddy's car window. A face with windshield eyes and a headlight nose peered back at him from down the railroad tracks. It was the face of a streamliner train coming from Atlanta heading south to Savannah, Ga.. Alarm bells rang and cars lined up behind the zebra-striped crossing gates. Steel wheels clattered over iron rails and hot air swirled around the long flowing lines of silver passenger cars. It was the "Nancy Hanks" passing by Crooks Crossing. The hot swirling wind reduced his once wide eyes to narrow slits. Through these slits he watched waiters in white chef's hats serving coffee to passengers in the dining cars. I remember it because I was that kid. Crooks Crossing has long since vanished. In its place is a no name crossing. No name trains come and go in and out of Atlanta and kids don't watch them anymore.

"LOOK OUT!" shouts Puddin. "You damn near hit him."

I slam on the breaks and we come to a tire screeching halt in a cloud of dust. In the rear view mirror, I see a boy standing alone on the road thumbing a ride.

"I swear I didn't see him," I tell Puddin in amazement.

"No wonder. I can tell you're off day dreaming somewhere."

"Maybe we ought to pick him up. After all, I did almost hit him."

"Ain't picking up a hitchhiker," she says. "He's probably a thief, murderer or worse."

"Look at him. He's no murderer. He's probably a college kid going home."

He starts running toward the car. A yellow and black plaid scarf wraps around his neck with its ends dangling in front of his tan coat. Flaps from his black-furry cap hang down like basset hound ears. Swinging from his hand is a small red canvas bag with a bull dog's face on its side.

"We gotta pick him up," I plead.

"He's just a kid," she admits. Maybe it'll be all right to ask where he's going. But if we pick him up, don't blame me if he kills us."

I back up the car, roll the window down and wave him on. A broad smile comes over his face and he starts running toward us flailing the bull-dog face bag in the air.

"Lord knows what we're in for," says Puddin.

The words are barely out of her mouth when the boy's smiling face, panting a cloudy winter's breath, appears in the open window.

"Hi, I'm going to College Hill. Mind if I hitch a ride?" he asks in an almost breathless voice. His facial expression hungers for a ride and a chance to get out of the cold.

"Get in," I say. "We're going I-75 south. We'll pass by the College Hill exit.."

"Awesome," he says as he opens the rear door, tosses the bag onto the seat and plops down beside it.

Puddin looks at the bulldog face on the bag and asks. "Do you go to the University of Georgia? We graduated from there and love those dogs. I think Uga is the bulldog mascot's name."

"Uh no," he says squirming nervously in his seat. "I just use this bulldog bag to get rides. I don't graduate high school till June."

"What's your name?" asks Puddin.

"Rusty ... Rusty Figly." he answers.

"Figly, Figly, hmm," Puddin murmurs. "You wouldn't be kin to Rufus Figly would you?"

"Yep, he was my dad."

His answer jolts my memory. I remember Rufus from the summer of 1960 when I sold peaches in Haynesville. He was a very popular insurance salesman who worked for Charity Life Insurance Co.. Must've sold life insurance to almost everyone in Haynesville. He had married Amybelle and moved to Macon. I can't believe we have just picked up their son.

"How's your dad doing?" I ask.

"He's dead. Had a heart attack a year ago."

"NO! Rufus dead. I'm sorry to hear that."

"You knew my daddy?"

"We sure did," says Puddin. "We knew your dad and mother when they lived in Haynesville. How's your mother doing?"

"Not good. That's why I'm going to see her."

I see his head bowed in the rear view mirror as if in prayer. The moaning tone in his voice tells me something bad is wrong with his mother Amybelle. I know Puddin will get to the bottom of it before we get to the College Hill exit.

"How's your mama taking his death?" Puddin asks, turning in the seat to face Rusty. No easy task for a woman of her immense size. She heaves her hefty arm over the seat and pats his knee. Rusty responds to her tenderness and begins pouring his heart out.

"Mama broke down at Daddy's funeral. Started kicking the coffin and hollering he'd been the Grim Reaper who caused the death of a man I never heard of called Leafy. She also said he'd caused lots of people to die too. I know Daddy could never do that. They took her away. She's been in the College Hill Mental Hospital a year now."

I couldn't help but notice how cold Puddin had taken his words. She knows Amybelle was telling the truth. Too bad no one listened to Amybelle when she was trying to explain what was going on in Haynesville. But then again, who would have listened to the words of a woman driven insane by her guilt? Guilt caused by the fact she had known what was going on in Haynesville and had done nothing about it.

"Who's been taking care of you?" Puddin asks.

"Matty's Foster home. It used to bother me when Matty fell asleep with her eyes open until I found out she's blind. I'm used to it now. You'd never know she's blind. She takes good care of us. Makes mighty fine biscuits too. She don't mind me hitch-hiking to see Mama. Besides, I'll be back before dark."

"You're a fine boy to care about your mother," says Puddin patting him on the knee again. "Let me tell you, your daddy had nothing to do with Leafy's death. Anybody in Haynesville will tell you Leafy's death was an accident. He died in the cotton gin fire. He must've just loaded chicken coops full of white leggings on his truck when he'd seen the fire's light in the sky. That old abandoned gin had to be in full blaze when he'd gotten there. Story goes he'd driven his truck too close to the gin and the flames caught the coops on fire. Next morning, they found his charred body dangling from the truck. Some say he might've made it if his boot laces hadn't tangled in the chicken coops."

"WOW!. That's a scary story. I can see why Daddy wouldn't have anything to do with that."

"You're right. He wouldn't," Puddin assures him. "I can't imagine why your mother would feel your dad had anything to do with Leafy's death."

I know Puddin's story is a lie. Leafy had been murdered.. Amybelle and Rufus knew it too. And now Amybelle's nervous breakdown has locked Haynesville's secret in her forever. I can't help but wonder how Rufus really died..

Ahead is the exit sign to College Hill. I'm not about to put Rusty out on the highway. **I'm taking him to The College Hill Mental Hospital and we're going to see Amybelle.**

Chapter 2

The Rainbow Inn

It's now late in the shank of noon as we leave the hospital and begin our 35 mile drive back to I-75. The sky is clear and the sunlight dances happily above the leafless trees. Our visit with Rusty's mother Amybelle was miserable. Gone is the wild spirit I saw in her sixteen years ago when I sold peaches in Haynesville. All that's left is a hunched over vegetable planted in a straight back chair. She looked older than her natural years of around forty. I had stood silent while Rusty rushed over and grabbed his mother's hand.

"Mother I've some old friends here to see you."

Amybelle ignored his words and remained a lifeless mindless body unaware of anything going on around her. Her head, crowned by a thin gray bun, did not turn to greet us. Unblinking lids offered little shelter to her glazed eyes staring into space. Thin fragile arms flowed like melted candle wax from her hunched over shoulder down to her withered hands folded in her lap. The sucking in and puffing out of her emaciated cheeks with each breath was the only human trait that remained. I watch Rusty take her in his arms anticipating a joyous hug. He was neither repulsed by her withered form nor openly displeased that no arms had wrapped around him pressing him to his mother's breast. He'd spoken like she'd heard every word he was saying.. "Mother," he repeated. I've brought you some old friends."

Rusty offered no explanation why his mother had not responded. There was no need. It was obvious Amybelle was gone. But there had been a time when she was very much alive. **I'll never forget that time.**

I had just graduated from The University of Georgia June 1960 and decided to spend the summer selling peaches to the snowbirds migrating north on 41 Hwy to escape the Florida's summer heat. So, early one morning, I gassed up my pick-up truck and drove south into Georgia peach country where I only planned to stay a few weeks. That truck was a beauty dented in all the right places with a dingy red finish splotched brown by the the Georgia sun. The trip had taken me through one small town after the other each with Welcome and Come Back Again signs. Speed limit signs made me slow down and speed up all day long. Towards evening, the sun light began to flicker through the tall Georgia pines causing their shadows to get longer and longer across 41 Hwy until it was dark. Snowbirds disappeared into motels for the night leaving me alone under a moonless sky. Animal eyes speckled in the truck's headlights as I drove through the darkness. Suddenly, in front of me came a weird aberration. It was an electrified bird with a big smile on its face standing by the Hwy. Its form blurred by the film of splattered bugs on my windshield. As I got closer, it became obvious this electrified creature was a neon sign on an iron pole advertising the Blue Bird Motel. A welcome sight for I was about to fall asleep at the wheel. The parking lot was a gravel pit. The truck's tires sent the gravel flying through the air making a cracking sound as it splattered off the motels front walls and the truck's fenders finally stopped rattling when it bounced to a stop. The motel was not very inviting and was quite ugly. Years of flying gravel had pockmarked the blue stuccoed room fronts which were lined up side-by-side and had a number on each door. An air conditioner protruded from each window. Their drain water's drip had nourished weeds under each window. A sign on the end room was marked office. One ring from the office bell summoned an old stooped shouldered humped back woman to the door. Her form, silhouetted against a faint light coming from a black-white TV in the background, was ghostly. Eyes, magnified by thick glasses perched on

her nose, studied me as she chewed on a snuff wad puckered in her left cheek. After sneering at me for a while, she finally spoke in a deep raspy voice. The kind of voice scorched by cigarette smoking and a long past woman's change of life.

"Yeah, yeah, what do you want?" she asked.

"I would like a room for the night."

"Why you ain't more than a child." Her magnified eyes threw daggers stabbing me to the bone as she spoke. "What you doing boy running from home?"

"No ma'am I'm down here to sell peaches."

"Don't need none," she said about to slam the door in my face. In a reflex jerky motion, I stuck my leg in the doorway to keep it from closing.

"No, you don't understand. I'm gonna sell left over peaches on 41 Hwy. to the snowbirds. Are there any orchards around here?"

"Lordy, I do reckon so, but Mr. Buck Mathas has them all. Son you done found the peach belly of the whole U.S of A. "

"That's what I'm looking for."

Her tone mellowed a bit after we'd talked a while. She even began to ease the pressure off my leg stuck in the door. Then her magnified eyes squinted at my truck in the parking lot and she asked, "you sporting a woman?"

"No ma'am I ain't."

"Humph, give me two dollars. You got a room."

I gave her two dollars and was rewarded with a key attached to an eight inch long piece of broom handle. Since there was no number on it, I asked "which room's mine?"

"Don't matter. That key fits them all. Pick whatever you like. They'll all be empty till the Rainbow let's out."

"I'll take room one." Now that I was an official guest, I thought it proper to introduce myself. "My name's Poon. What's yours?"

"Ain't got none. At least none you'd be interested in." She paused a while and began laughing. "POON, POON," she howled from a toothless, tobacco spitting hole of a mouth in her face. "How'd you get that name?"

"My baby name. I've been stuck with it all my life. Everybody's got a name. Don't matter what it is. What's yours?"

"Call me Madam," she answered spitting a snuff wad out the door. I marked its landing so not to step in it. "Folks around here call me that. Least behind my back anyways."

Without knowing what Madam meant at that time, I responded. "Madam it is. Madam I'm hungry. Been driving all day. Had nothing to eat. And I'm lost."

"Hells bells boy you gotta be a blithering idiot. You're telling me you don't know where you're at."

"Yeah."

"Boy you're in Haynesville. Haynesville's where you're at."

Her words meant nothing. I hadn't known half the towns I drove through that day. I was thirsty and hungry and wanted a place to eat.

"Is there a place to eat around here?"

"Ain't nothing open but the Rainbow this time a night. But I'd stay outta there if I was you. It's a devil's den infested with demons."

Her words made no sense to me. Food was all I wanted.

"Does this den place have anything to eat?" I asked.

"Yeah. Barbeque ribs and all."

"Well, where's this place?"

"It's back a ways over younder," she said waving her knobby fingers in no particular direction which prompted me to ask.

"Where's that?"

"You're a bustin' your britches for trouble ain't you boy?"

"No, I just wanna eat. Just tell me where's this place."

"Whooh doggies. Boy you're getting mighty uppity for one who's lost in these parts. Maybe a dose of the Rainbow will do you good."

"Yeah, yeah, where is it."

"Well, all you gotta do is go to that road younder," she said pointing to 41 Hwy. Do you see it?"

"I do."

"That goes to the Mathas Bros. Warehouse. When you see it, turn left and keep going around the square and across the railroad tracks. Keep going. You'll hear music that'll guide you to the Rainbow. I'm jabbered out. Night's air ah chillin' my bones. I'm-----

I interrupted her cause I was beginning to get worried about this devil's den. After all, I was in a strange place with a strange old lady talking about it. So I asked in a sheepish tone of voice low and studdery like.

"W-w-why are you calling this place a devil's den?"

"You'll see. Go there. You'll see. The Rainbow's doing the devil's work and it goes on in his den."

Madam was right. When I walked into the smoke filled Rainbow Inn that night a young girl was strutting barefooted back and forth atop the bar. Her long blond pony tail swished wildly in the air as she screamed at the top of her lungs in a voice that soared above the sultry blues tune playing on the jukebox.

"If a woman's all you want, whores will screw you good."

"Don't you think I ain't gone to whores to finish what sex you'd started," a man sitting at the bar screamed back at her through his beer foam coated lips drooping sadly under his mustache. His face had now retreated from her savage attack and hid behind a beer bottle sitting on the bar. Threads of coal black hair hung down from atop his head to mingle with the beads of sweat on his forehead. A loose tie knot, an unbuttoned shirt collar and curly chest hair made a comfortable nest for his chubby neck to nestle in.

"You ain't getting mine. Not a whiff." The girl responded thrusting her crotch into the man's face. "You gotta get a woman's head right 'fore you screw 'em," she said while picking a beer bottle off the bar and smashing it against the wall emphasizing her words. Splattered beer smeared the wall in a glistening star-burst white foam pattern which oozed down the wall making a puddle on the floor.

That had been my introduction to Amybelle the Rainbow Inn's waitress. And the man at the bar was Rufus Figly a life insurance salesman who had come from Macon to sell life insurance throughout the small south Georgia towns. From the looks of Rusty, Rufus had gotten Amybelle's head right after all.

Madam was right. The Rainbow Inn was the devil's den. I stayed at the Bluebird Motel and discovered why this old lady had been called Madam. She owned the only hot sheet motel in town. Night after night, when the Rainbow Inn closed, I watched the drunk farmers, pickers and loose women of the town stagger into its rooms.

For two weeks in June 1960, I picked and sold peaches in Haynesville. I watched in amazement how fast the pickers gathered peaches from the low pruned tree branches and placed them into buckets hanging around their necks on canvas straps. When their buckets were full, they dumped the peaches into bins carried on wagons pulled by tractors to the packing shed. The packing shed was nothing more than a waist high wooden platform mounted on a cement block foundation with a corrugated tin roof. This height made it easy to unload the bins from the wagons onto a long conveyer belt that transported the peaches between rows of shed workers. A water shower from over head hoses cleansed the peaches of pesticides and insects. Shed workers culled the peaches by selecting bad peaches from the good ones. Bad peaches were thrown onto the ground where pigs squealed and rooted them from the wet sandy soil. The next row of workers wrapped each individual good peach in purple colored tissue and placed it into a wooden crate. The last row hammered the crates shut, stamped them Mathas Orchards, and loaded them into the refrigerated railroad box cars at the shed's end. It was a sight to behold.

Old Peach Stand Along 41 Hwy

Mornings, I would drive my truck into the orchards and pick the peaches left behind by the pickers. They were free, because they would rot on the trees if no one picked them. Pickers always left wooden bushel baskets behind too. All I had to do was pick the peaches, put them in the baskets and load them onto my truck. Afternoons I would sell them from a stand beside 41 Hwy. Barefooted, dressed in faded blue jeans, and a frayed straw hat made me look like a poor farm boy. Snowbirds migrating north to escape the summer's heat bought so many peaches I had no idea where to hide the money. So I stuffed it into my truck's upholstery. By week's end, I had stuffed the ceiling, door panels, and both seats with dollar bills.

Watching Amybelle at the Rainbow Inn night after night had been an education in itself. Her let's do it eyes always kept the sex starved men sitting at the bar in a stir. I must admit, that blond pony tail swirling around her waist and breast spilling out of a cheap skimpy mail order bra, the thin white fabric waitress uniform stretched tight across her thighs to grope the groove between her firm buttocks stirred within me a longing for her body. But I knew my fantasy would never come true. Ostracized by Haynesville's so called decent people, the Rainbow Inn had become her home and everybody there loved her. How sad it must've been for them when she married Rufus and moved to Macon.

"Get off here Ive gotta go to the bathroom," commands Puddin. Her voice breaks the silence and puts me back in my present dismal place, our rolling tomb, the car.

"But there's nothing here," I explain. "We'll go to a rest stop?"

"No, I'll pee anywhere. Get off at this exit."

We exit off I-75 onto a narrow two lane road that eventually led to a box shaped restaurant with just enough paint left on its stucco exterior to show it was once white. What color it is now is anybody's guess. A flat roof makes it look like a giant out-house. Iva's Diner is painted in bold red letters on the huge front plate glass window.

"Stop here," says Puddin, "This place is bound to have a rest-room. Maybe we can eat here too."

"I don't know. This place may have a restroom, but I don't think I wanna eat here."

Reluctantly, I stop in the diner's empty parking lot which is small and dotted with grassy clumps growing through the cracks in its crumbling cement surface. Puddin flings open the car door allowing a cold winter's blast to greet my face. This is immediately followed by a squeaking sound from sweaty flesh sliding over the leather covered seat.

Rocking back and forth, she manages to get out of the car and with a grunt begins her characteristic waddle towards the diner's entrance. She pauses briefly to shake down her black and orange plaid wool skirt over her chubby knees. In front of her is the word 'OPEN', cut from an old quilt, hanging behind the diner's clear glass door. A cowbell's hollow clank announces our entrance as I open the door for her to enter the diner. We are immediately confronted by chrome rimmed stools and booths with cushions covered in red faded vinyl. . . all empty.

"Is anybody here." ask Puddin. Her voice is low since the place is small and anyone here will surely hear her bellowing voice.

"I'm here," comes a shrill, squealing voice from the kitchen. It was like the sound you'd hear from a car with bad breaks. "Yawl sit. I'm ah coming."

"I've gotta go to the bathroom," says Puddin. "But I ain't going till I see who or what goes with that voice."

I began toying with a greasy tattered plastic piece lying on the table to discover it's a menu. Through its greasy grimy surface, I see it's filled with orders for southern fried chicken, barbeque ribs and country fried ham dinners. All served with okra and succotash

"This place has got some good food," I tell Puddin.

My mouth is watering for some southern fried chicken when this babe pops out of the kitchen sporting orange hair wrapped in a purple scarf. Her head rotates back and forth scanning the room through white rimmed sunglasses looking for who's invaded her private domain. Spotting us, she hollers, "there yawl are." And marches over to our booth.

"Gimme that," she says snatching the menu from my hands. "You don't need no menu. Eggs, grits, toast is what I'm ah fixin' and that's what yawl are ah having. My name's Iva. I'll bring it right out." she says marching off to wherever she came from.

Puddin thinks nothing of Iva's rudeness and disappears behind a wooden door marked bathroom located beside our booth. You can hear the toilet's flushing sound loud and clear throughout the entire diner signaling Puddin's return to the booth.

"Bathroom's a green slimy mess," she complains. "Looks like no one's ever used it. For sure no one's ever cleaned it."

In a flash, our purple headed shrill talking waitress appears out of nowhere with our food. Puddin begins devouring her eggs and grits like a pig while our waitress hovers over us like a humming bird looking for nectar. She pours coffee in our cups after each sip we take and pays little attention to a cockroach scampering across the table to disappear into the wall.

"Well I'll be," she says calmly, "I just thought they were in the kitchen."

That's it. I'm done. The waitress spots my sudden distaste for the eggs and asked, "what's the matter son? Them eggs too ripe? I can get some mellow ones for you if you'd like."

"No," Puddin butts in, "Leave 'em. I'll eat 'em."

"Well alright hon. I'll bring you more grits if you need 'em. Got some good ham too."

Puddin cleans up my plate and moves on to a side order of ham and an extra helping of grits.

"More coffee?" ask the waitress waving a fresh brewed pot over the table.

"No," I answer. I was still wondering what a mellow egg would look like.

"Yeah," Puddin grunts, "pour me some."

Puddin's been at the trough now for over an hour. Glistening butter grease coats her chin. Grits dangle in chunks from the deep-fat furrows that were once the dainty corners of her mouth. The waitress stands watching Puddin trying to swipe the unsightly mess off her face with a wad of napkins.

"Need more napkins hon?"

"No, I'm done," Puddin answers throwing the napkin wad down onto the empty plate.

I can tell by the silly look on the waitress's face she wants to make a crack about Puddin's appetite and how her big fat butt fills the whole seat on one side of the booth. But she resists the temptation and simply says in a lovely toned sweet voice, "that'll be eight dollars please."

"Get much business out here?" I ask the waitress.

"A might," she answers.

"Seems like a town ought to be here somewhere."

"It was till I-75 killed it."

"What town was it?"

She ignores my question and keeps clearing the dirty dishes off the table, cradles them in her apron and disappears behind the kitchen's swinging doors. I thought my question would go unanswered till I heard the dishes crash into the sink and heard her say, "town was Pennyfield."

"Pennyfield, never heard of it," I answered in a loud voice so she could hear me above the sound from the dishes rattling in the sink.

"I was born and raised here," she goes on to say. Never thought I'd out live the town, but I have. Gotta stay here town or no town. Ain't got nowhere else to go. My daddy and mama built this diner and left it to me when they died. Running Iva's Diner is all I know how to do."

Iva's not alone. The construction of I-75 had sent many a small town to its doom. Before then U.S. 41 (previously known as The Dixie Hwy) was the main route taking snowbirds back and forth to Florida through Georgia. Towns like Pennyfield had thrived in the 50's-60's. Their colorful signs advertising motels and restaurants had been painted on barn roofs far north as Sault Ste. Marie, Michigan. Ranch style two story motels surrounded by Shamrock green St. Augustine grass and crystal clear swimming pools flourished. Restaurants had gotten bigger and fancier with eight foot long crisp salad bars and fine southern home cooking. Gas stations sold everything you could imagine: Talmadge sugar cured hams, pecan candy log rolls, dried dead shellac painted baby alligators, wooden tomahawks adorned in feathers and porcelain dolls made in Japan. Unfortunately, these towns became places of depression and despair when I-75 was completed between Sault Ste. Marie, Michigan and Tampa, Florida. No longer was U.S. 41 the main route carrying snowbirds through these towns north in summer from Florida and south in winter to Florida. And no longer did the snowbird's money support these towns' economy.

Commercial peach production dating back to the 1860s was also dying a slow agonizing death due to disease that threatened to kill the peach trees and the developing social change in the country known as LBJ's "Great Society". Pickers had rather go on welfare than spend hot August days in the orchards picking peaches. As the peach industry began to fail, so did the soft touch and eye for the shady green color necessary to harvest a peach so delicious its pulp would fall away from the seed. These had become known as "Georgia freestones". Now the few peaches that were being harvested were too firm and too green for the pulp to fall away from the seed. These less flavorful peaches became know as "clingstones" and were less sought after adding even further economic failure to these towns.

All of these conditions forced those who could to flee these towns leaving behind the scattered remains of their businesses . . . burned down motels, gas stations naked without their pumps, and vandalized restaurants scarred by boarded up broken windows. Like Iva some people had no choice but to remain in Haynesville because all they knew how to do was operate the farms and businesses handed down to them from generation to generation. They were rooted in the land and were known by such family names as The Wilson's Farm, Mathas Orchards and Childers Drug Store. Like the generations before them, they had to stay and survive no matter what the sacrifice, so in death the next generation would inherit the land and do the same even if it had to be done in a desperate way. Puddin and I lived through these times and witnessed these town's devastation caused by I-75. Memories of which, I'm sure, prompted Puddin to say, "I've promised Mother **I'll never let Haynesville disappear like Pennyfield."**

Chapter 3

The Peach Orchard Meeting

We leave Pennyfield around 3:30 p.m. and continue our trip down I-75 that cement ribbon to Hell. Over the past seven years, Puddin has turned into the kind of woman you'd meet there too. No heart and a body like a stack of tires. One fat roll indistinguishable from the other. Demons speak through her body of

Haynesville Peach Tree

rubbing fabric, grunts and whistling nose hairs. Their excrements form dirt rings around her neck and sewer water drains from her arm pits. Yet, like an ugly pet, there are moments when I find myself attached to her and even in love with her. It's now hard to believe she's the girl I met in the peach orchard beneath a June nervous sky. A sky that could burst into thunder and lightening and a down pour of drenching rain at any time. It'd been fitting weather to sow my seeds of greed. I first saw her from a distance milling amongst the peach trees. Their limbs heavy with fresh fruit begging to be picked. I watched her long slender legs sweeping back and forth under her thin cotton apron drenched in peach juice as she climbed the wooden steps leading up to the packing shed.

I watched her slender fingers tenderly fondling the peaches sprawled out on the long table in front of her. Her movements had been so sensual that it stirred within me fantasies of my tongue plowing her crevice until it disappeared into the furrow between her thighs. I had to meet this beautiful girl. So, it all began with a simple **introduction. . .**

"My name's Poon what's yours?"

My words sent her frayed straw hat bobbing up-and-down like a bird searching for food on a creek bottom. I couldn't help but notice how her long sleeve shirt was buttoned tightly around her neck and wrist to keep out the invisible peach fuzz. Peach juice dripped off the table forming a puddle around her sneakers. Whoever she is, she is no stranger to the peach orchards. I never thought she would answer my question until she said with a giggle.

"Hush your mouth. That's not really your name."

Perhaps she had been too shy to look at me, for her brown eyes remained fixed on the peaches in front of her. But why should she look at me? After all, I was no handsome prince appearing majestically from the orchards. An un-made bed would've been a more accurate description of my appearance. My greasy red hair made my head look like an overflowing backed up toilet bowl. Freckles mixed with zits dotted my face. Two small round eyes astride a pegged nose had stimulated my mother to give me a baby name Poon. My unwashed jeans and T-shirt matted on my skinny body like wads of Spanish Moss. And to make matters worse, I had yet to discover under arm deodorant so my arm pits reeked with an out house odor. None of this mattered now. I was a bird dog on the hunt and before me stood my prey.

"Yeah my name's really Poon. What's yours," I asked again.

She didn't answer. It was painfully obvious that I had not impressed her. She just wiped a lock of her shoulder length auburn hair from her forehead and kept on fondling the peaches. I hoped she would look up at me and our eyes would meet. But she didn't. I stood next to her resisting my temptation to rub my knee against her thigh when her sparkling brown eyes lifted up from beneath the straw hat and looked at me as she asked . . .

"Are you from around here?"

"No, I'm from Jonesboro up by Atlanta. I'm here selling peaches to get money for school. I'm going to The Medical College of Georgia this fall," I said proudly.

"You've gotta be kidding?" she squealed like she'd just met an old friend.

"No, I ain't."

"I'll be there too in nursing school. My name's Puddin. Puddin Mathas."

Those words still ring in my ears today, for I had just met the one and only daughter of Mr. Buck Mathas Jr. the wealthiest peach farmer in Orchard County. A meeting that planted in me seeds of greed so strong that they still haunt me today. Marry his daughter and, who knows, someday I would inherit his orchards and be the richest man in Orchard County.

"What a beautiful name. How'd you get it?" I asked.

"I'll never tell," she answered, "but it has to do with my grandmother's rice pudding."

"Well, we've both got one thing in common. . . funny names," I said with a broad smile on my face. She hadn't thought my comment funny so I went on to explain, "Puddin and Poon does have a good ring to it. Don't you think?" And that's how our meeting began.

The day's heat had eased a bit and the air stirred a might. We'd been too busy talking to notice the conception of a thunder storm brewing over head. Too busy talking to feel its baby mist. Too busy talking to see its infantile dark storm cloud toddling overhead grow into an adolescence that could no longer be ignored. Now all grown up it let loose an ear piercing lightning crack followed by a sweeping rain that came from all directions at once.

"My truck," I sputtered through the rain water streaming down my face. "Let's get in my truck."

Puddin faced with either getting struck by lightning or drenched in the rain's down pour had no choice but to follow me into my truck. There we found a private world hidden behind a curtain of cascading rain waterfalls pouring down over the truck's windows.

"That lightning was close. Look at me I'm soaking wet," said Puddin.

"Are you cold?" I whispered as I put my arms around her.

"No," she answered squirming in her seat.

It was not a resistive squirm. Not a squirm that told me she was uncomfortable about my arms being around her, but one that said she was nervous about what might be coming next. It was as if she knew about the war raging within me. The war between me and my hormones. I already lost the battle by not thrusting my hand underneath her apron, but I won the war by kissing her.

"Stop," she giggled.

I ignored her giggling because a considerable discomfort had begun to develop in the crotch of my tight blue jeans for which I had no immediate solution. Unbuttoning my fly would be too obvious. Spreading my legs apart had only increased my discomfort. Just when I thought there would be no escape, it extended itself down my left pant leg. I groaned a sigh of relief at its new found freedom. Sensing it unwise to pursue my sexual exploits further I asked,

"Wanna go to a movie tonight? We can take my truck to Macon."

"I can't. Daddy would never let me go. Besides it's Wednesday a prayer meeting night. I gotta go to church."

"Prayer meeting's fine with me. What time?"

"Six o'clock at the Baptist Church across the street from where I live. on Wayside Street."

"Wayside Street, Yeah I know where that is. I'll meet you there."

I couldn't believe it. I just met The Peach King's daughter and we had already been making out in my truck. In my excitement, I failed to notice the storm had passed taking with it the cascading rain curtain from the truck's windows. Our once private world was now exposed in the sunlight and I heard a big [WHUMP] noise. It sounded like something big hit the truck. The [WHUMP, WHUMP] noise continued and sounded like someone was pounding on the truck's roof with their fist.

"GET OUT! YOU HEAR! GET OUT!

"DADDY!" shrieked Puddin in terror as she lunged out the door to disappear behind the truck.

[WHUMP, WHUMP!] The sound had now begun to come from the front of the truck where a beet-red faced man stood with a jack-o-lantern looking head staring at me through the windshield. Its candle lit and its eyes on fire.

"Git outta here! Better not catch you messing with my daughter again. You hear me **BOY?"**

These thunderous words had come from frozen lips that'd never moved. Instead, he'd growled them around a cigar clenched between his teeth. Panic had stretched every fiber in my body to the breaking point causing me to floorboard the accelerator and let out the clutch. The rear view mirror had shown it all. The truck's spinning tires splattering dirt in Puddin's daddy's beet red face. A sight I thought would ruin my chances of ever seeing her again. But, I was not about to give up and went to the Baptist Church that evening hoping to see her. There I paced back and forth in the front church yard waiting anxiously for her to come out of her house across the street. Her front door never opened and she never came to church that night.

I was about to get in my truck and leave when I saw Fussel and George come prancing out the church front door. They spotted me at once and came running over to the truck. Both were wide eyed and surprised to see me. I had met them yesterday in the orchards while picking peaches and knew I was in for trouble. Both had been born in Haynesville and, now, as teenagers around sixteen years old, were in the process of growing up there too. Fussel, was Cleve Elderidge's son and George was Tiny Childers' son. Everybody knew them because Fussel's daddy owned the funeral home while George's daddy owned the Drug Store.

"What are you doing here? Don't tell me you're going to the prayer meeting," said George giggling under his breath while Fussel stood gawking at me as if expecting a silly answer.

"I'm looking for Puddin. Have you seen her?"

"You don't mean Buck's daughter do you?" George asked. -

"Yeah, Puddin. Have you seen her?"

"You gotta be kidding," Fussel butted in, "ain't no boy gonna get any of that. I hear tell if you go to her house Buck will meet you at the door with a shotgun in his hand."

"He's right," agreed George. "We call it redneck birth control."

Besides you don't need her when you can get parking religion like we do."

"Yeah, we're real sanctified," said Fussel. "Wednesday prayer meeting nights are when we get our religion in the parking lot. Wanna join us?"

"Join what? Is the prayer meeting in the parking lot?""

"No, no you don't understand. When it gets dark and while everybody's in church singing we're out screwing in the parking lot.

"Yeah," said George. "We put them cars to good use. Come on we'll show you how we get through these long prayer meetings."

"Who do we fix him up with?" Fussel asked George.

"Roxy James, that's who. She loves parking lot religion. Poon do you know her?"

"No. I don't know any girls down here but Puddin."

"Don't matter. We'll get her in the Judge's Buick for you. There's plenty of room in there. He parks next to the window with the big cross on it. You can hear Rev. Boswell's voice real good from there."

I looked at the shadowy outlines of the cars in the parking lot and sure enough there it was the Judge's Buick with big chrome grill teeth grinning at me from under the multicolored stained glass window with the cross on it.

"Don't roll up the windows," said George in a broken voice ravaged by adolescent hormones.

"He's right," Fussel agreed. "You gotta hear the praying, preaching and singing," he said in a serious tone of voice like he had just given me the secrets of King Tut's Tomb. "Listen to me so you don't mess up and ruin the whole thing for us all. Her dress has gotta be off by the opening prayer. Get her titties out during the hymn singing and panties off before the preaching starts."

"Yeah, yeah," Fussel interrupted all excited by George's instructions. "You gotta keep up with the preaching while you're doing it. Hell, we're listening better than any of them do-good church people. Cause you gotta be through before the preaching stops."

"Right on," said George. "I gotta warn you. Don't let no burning in Hell preaching make your dick limp. We're used to Rev. Boswell's preaching and screw through it all with no problem. The last hymn's important cause you both gotta be dry, dressed and outta the car by the last verse. Here's the most important thing. Be standing in the front yard when they sing the Benediction. That'll make it look like you'd been in church the whole time and had just come out the door to stand in the yard."

I couldn't believe my ears. That was the wildest thing I ever heard. No way was I gonna do that. During their detail instructions, a thunderstorm began to ruffle the leaves in the oak trees towering over the church. Then a lightning ball of fire struck from out of nowhere and lit up the tree next to us in an eerie glow which sizzled down the ivy vines entwined around the tree's trunk to the ground. Smoke puffed from the burning vines and the smell of burning leaves filled the musty humid night's air. Stunned by this sight, Fussel sank to his knees and shook his fist at the black heavens and yelped,

"GOD YOU MISSED ME!"

Fussel's sacrilegious act upset George so bad he began shouting at Fussel, **"SHUT UP! HE CAN STILL HIT US!"**

The lightning crack brought people scampering out of the church to roll up their car windows before it rained.

"Ain't gonna be any parking lot religion tonight," said Fussel. "With the car's windows rolled up and the church windows shut, we can't hear Rev. Boswell's divine guidance. We'll get caught with our pants down for sure."

There was nothing else to do but seek shelter in the church in case it rained. What a mistake that had been. Thank goodness we sat on the back pew because Fussel leaned over towards me and whispered in my ear, "George's so horney he's done near poked ever thing in sight. Chickens ain't even safe."

I ducked my head down low to my knees and hoped no one had heard him above the organ music and singing. George had also leaned over toward Fussel to hear what he was whispering to me.

"Ain't so," George whispered in my ear. "I ain't never poked a chicken. Poked a lot of watermelons, but no chickens. Nothing better than plugging gushy warm melons that'd been in the sun all day. I could poke one right now. Poon do you like plugging watermelons?"

I never answered that question and Puddin never came to the prayer meeting that night either.

Early next morning before the July flies had begun to sing, I pushed my legs into some blue jeans from the pile of cloths lying on the floor at the Bluebird Motel. Put on a white cotton T-shirt and stuffed my bare feet into my tennis shoes for I was going back to Jonesboro. Last sound I remember hearing that day in Haynesville was a loud pop from the Bluebird Motel's wooden door slamming shut behind me.

Driving back to Jonesboro I couldn't help but reflect back on all that had happened to me in just a few weeks. My happiest thought was that of Puddin for I knew we would see each other again in school this fall and return again to our secret world. I'll never forget our first date which had led me into **The Peach King's private domain and Haynesville's twisted society.**

Chapter 4

Grandma's Funeral

My first week in medical school began with a bang. I came face-to-face with a dead body called a cadaver preserved in formaldehyde lying on a shiny stainless steel table for dissection. I sat on a high stool around the table making it easy to lean over and cut the clay-like bloodless flesh. Through a filmy veil of tears from the formaldehyde fumes stinging my eyes, I uncovered the endless tangle of blood vessels and nerves.

Puddin and I had only been in school two weeks when we had our first date. We had gone to the movies seven o'clock Sunday evening where she insisted on immediately finding a telephone. Even now, I shudder to think it all began with **an innocent phone call. .**

"I've gotta call Mother," she said as her eyes shifted nervously around the lobby looking for a telephone.

"But the movie is about to start," I said.

"It's silly I know, but I promised I would call her every Sunday evening at seven o'clock to let her know I'm alright. She'll be worried if I don't call her right away."

"There's a phone," I said pointing towards the ladies restroom.

"Good, I'll only be a minute."

While she spoke to her mother, I stood in the lobby watching couples balancing popcorn bags and sodas in their hands as they disappeared through the double doors into the theater's darkness. The movie's amplified dialogue and music got louder and softer each time the doors opened and closed. We were missing the movie's beginning, but it made no difference to Puddin. She kept talking to her mother. So I went over to her and noticed tears glittering in her eyes. Tears even glistened on the telephone's carbon black surface. Her head tossing in a NO! NO! motion as she hung up the phone. It was obvious something terrible had happened. Not knowing what to do, I simply asked,

"What's wrong?"

"Grandmother died. Take me to the bus station. I've gotta go home. I've gotta go NOW!"

"Not now, it's too late," I said trying to calm the panic in her voice. Wait till tomorrow. I'll drive you home. We'll leave first thing in the morning."

"Would you do that?"

"Sure, I'll stay at the Bluebird Motel."

"Hush your mouth. You'll stay at my house."

"You gotta be kidding. Your daddy would never allow that. You remember how mad he'd gotten when he caught us in my truck? The sight of us together would throw him into a rage. I don't even wanna think about it."

"Daddy's mad at you. That's for sure. Maybe you best put me on the bus."

"No, I'm not gonna do that. I'm not gonna let you be alone on a bus at a time like this. I'll take you home in the morning. If your daddy gets mad, I'll handle it somehow."

"Poon, you're so mature. I've never met anyone like you before."

"I'm just doing what's right that's all." What a lie. What I really wanted to do was get in good with her daddy The Peach King of Orchard County---Mr. Buck Mathas Jr.. Taking his daughter home for his mother's funeral seemed like a good way to do that too. I had seen his kind before and knew he'd be a rough brash man with dogmatic opinions about everything. He probably never finished high school. I was sure his grammar, made even worse by a thick Southern drawl, would be awful. Raised a farmer, he would wear bib jeans, flannel shirts, and brogan shoes. Only an impeccable white hat, that could even be worn on New York's Wall Street, would mark him wealthy. Those who dealt with him in business would soon learn he was a common horse-sense genius who understood nothing but cash money and a hand shake.

Words like credit and mortgage would not be in his vocabulary. Mr. Mathas was indeed rich. His orchards extended far as the eye could see. And his peach packing sheds, spread throughout his orchards, were too numerous to count. MATHAS ORCHARDS in bold letters identified his refrigerated box cars rolling on his railroad tracks through his orchards shipping his peaches across the U.S.A. and Canada. All his money had made him the ruler of his domain. He was the undisputed Peach King of Orchard County. I was convinced whoever married Puddin would someday inherit his powerful empire. And now Puddin's grandmother's death had given me a chance to strike at the Peach King's heart.

Next morning on our drive to Haynesville Puddin's grief stricken face of swollen eyes, weepy nose and quivering lips showed she loved her grandmother dearly and was devastated by her death. Her grief touched me so I asked,

"Why do you love your grandmother so much? Or would you rather not talk about it right now?"

"No I don't mind," she answered in a somber voice. Then paused a moment too emotional to speak, closed her eyes, and slipped back into her own private grieving world filled with sobbing and tear soaked cheeks.

"Grandma loved me. When I was a child, she would hold me in her arms till my hurt went away." Choking on her words, she became painfully silent again. I dared not disturb her for fear of making her grief even worse. Instead, I began thinking about her mother and what kind of woman she would be to marry Mr. Mathas.. I pictured her a plain, middle aged woman with little intelligence. Too engrossed in her knitting and quilting to speak her mind. Satisfying her husband would be her only life's ambition.

Later that afternoon we turned left off 41 Hwy onto Wayside Street bumping over the railroad tracks leading to the Mathas Bros. Warehouse. It was a bee hive of activity. Empty peach crates and sacks of fertilizer were being unloaded from the railroad boxcars at the loading dock. The warehouse was made of black splotched cinder block walls and a corrugated tin roof. It was a real eye sore. But inside was everything a farmer needed for a successful crop. We stopped at Haynesville's one and only stop light which hung over a busy intersection cluttered with colorful signs directing snowbirds to motels and restaurants. Already the snowbirds were beginning to migrate from their northern homes to Florida for the winter. The two gas stations katy cornered across from each other at the intersection were crammed with out-of-state cars. Their occupants, dressed in Bermuda shorts and polo shirts, milled about the water fountain stretching their legs. Gas station attendants, dressed in crisp white uniforms, scurried around the cars wiping windshields, waving rags and oily dipsticks in the air.

"Daddy's truck is parked at the warehouse," says Puddin. "He won't be home."

"Thank God," I sighed in relief.

The stoplight turned green and I drove on down Wayside Street slowly like I was trying to sneak into a dirty movie. When there it was, the place where I had seen Fussel and George only two months ago. . .The Haynesville Baptist Church. Across the street is Puddin's house. A red shingled roof white clapboard house nestled in a group of oak trees. There leaves colored between a Summer's green and a Fall's gold. When I turned into the driveway, I chuckled discretely at the sight of the front door wondering if Mr. Mathas would've really met me there with a shotgun in his hand.

"Drive around back," she said. "We're gonna park at the back door. It'll make it easy to unload our suitcases.

I followed her instructions and drove around the half-moon circle gravel driveway behind the house and parked in front of two brick steps leading up to a screened-in back porch. My heart began to pound so forcefully it sent painful throbbing pulses through my chest, neck and brain. This was no ordinary house I was about to enter. It was the Peach King's Castle. A realization that magnified my senses of sight, sound and smell to a fever pitch. Through the screen, I could see the porch was really a laundry room complete with the smell of clorox bleach in the air, a white chipped enamel washing machine and an ironing board with its cover scorched charcoal brown in spots. There was no clothes dryer which explained the four shirts hanging on a clothesline in the backyard. A yellow bug light dangled from the ceiling on a frayed electric cord ready to illuminate the battleship gray pine board floor at the pull of its bead chain. I opened the screen door for Puddin to enter the porch which stretched a long spring on the door used to keep it shut. It made a twanging sound and the door closed with a snapping bang

"Puddin is that you?" asked someone in a silky smooth voice coming from somewhere in the house.

"Yes, Mother it's me. I want you to meet someone," Puddin said pulling me into the house where a tall woman was standing in the kitchen. Her shapely hips tightly wrapped in a black velvet skirt slit up the side so as to show her silk stocking high above the knee. A pearl necklace played in the bountiful cleavage between her breast. Perhaps this beauty Queen from the past was Puddin's mother, but no way was she Mr. Mathas's wife.

"Mother I want you to meet Poon Rutherford. He's just started medical school. He was kind enough to bring me home for Grandma's funeral. Isn't that wonderful?"

This creature before me whose cold and expressionless face appeared more mannequin than human turned toward me. Her velvet skirt rustled and diamonds sparkled from her fingers. Slowly she removed a cigarette from between her thickly lipstick painted ruby red lips. Wispy smoke oozed from her mouth as her brown eyes assaulted me in a full frontal attack from a fortress of black, false eyelashes.

"You are who?" she asked.

Too intimidated to fire back anything more profound than my name I blurted out. “I’m Poon Rutherford,” I said holding out my hand to shake hers in a friendly greeting.

“Glad to meet you I guess” she responded to my friendly greeting and shook my hand. “My friends call me Vivian. You can too if you like. Yawl must be tired and hungry after that long drive from Augusta. Fix yourselves something to eat. I’ve gotta meet Cleve at the church about some last minute funeral arrangements. So, I’ve gotta run. Why don’t yawl go eat with Fussel. He’s by himself at the funeral home. Food’s not so good there since his mother died. Get Puddin to tell you how we used to go to the funeral home and talk about how good the deceased looked and how good her fried chicken smelled cooking up-stairs. Buck’s devastated by his mother’s death. He’s disappeared. Locked in his office at the warehouse I suspect. Grandma Mathas is in the funeral home. Yawl go see her. Cleve’s done a wonderful job on her. This is his first big funeral. Yawl’ll be delighted to see how he’s redone the church inside. I’ve always told Cleve he’s wasting his time down here when he could be making big Atlanta money.” She kept talking as she grabbed a black velvet jacket off the dining room chair.

“He’s expecting a big crowd. But we don’t have to worry. We’ve reserved seats down front so we can see everything.”

Sounded to me like we were going to a Broadway Show rather than a funeral. Her red painted finger nails disappeared into the velvet jacket and when they reappeared from its sleeves they clawed her shoulder length black hair from around its collar. “Bye-bye,” she said to the sound of a flurry of spiked high heel shoes clicking across the back porch wooded floor and down the brick steps to her car. Again I heard the twanging sound from the spring as the back porch door opened and the BANG as it slammed shut. Her exit had been anything but quiet. I was dumbfounded. Puddin's mother was nothing like I expected.

"Get ready," said Puddin, "we're going to the funeral home."

"You mean right now?"

"Yes. You don't have to go if you don't want to."

"No, no. I'll go. I wanna be with you. That's why I'm here. To be with you."

"You'll be in the front bedroom. Put your things in there."

Like her mother, Puddin's house was nothing like I expected. The hardwood floors creaked and sagged under my feet with each step I took to the front bedroom. The bedroom door yawned a muffled squeak as I opened and closed it. A single chest of drawers rattled against the wall in cadence with my footsteps. Even the ragged hook-rug on the floor skidded under my feet. The only thing that hadn't moved was the orange and red patch-work quilt covering the bed. Venetian blinds, covering the front bedroom window, dimmed the shrinking day light in the room as it was getting late in the afternoon. Gray bands of light glittered through the blind's wooden slats and flickered across my chest as I peered out the bedroom window. And there it was across the street. The Haynesville Baptist Church pointing to heaven. Pointed stained glass windows, high-pitched roof and towering steeple all pointed to heaven. Already I began feeling the Grandmother's presence who'd soon be lying there across the street. I

put on my black suit and tie for my visit with the deceased Grandmother knowing full well she would not care what I was wearing. I went into the living room looking for Puddin and was surprised to see that a black leather covered sofa and two side chairs were the only furniture in the room. Each faced the front window with a view of the church. There were no curtains, rugs, pictures or lamps. I couldn't believe a man of Mr. Mathas' wealth would have such a modest home. Suddenly, Puddin appeared in the living room and said nothing about my suit and tie. She was still wearing the same green skirt and white blouse she had on during our trip. She barely looked at me and said, "Come on let's go."

I'm not fond of dead people and I dreaded seeing the deceased Grandmother. But it had to be done. I could not miss this opportunity to get in good with the Mathas family. And Mr. Mathas, how could he still be mad at me after I brought his daughter home for his mother's funeral? And how could he be mad at me after I paid my respects to his mother in the funeral home? He couldn't. I already began feeling like a rich Mathas family member.

The funeral home is an old southern mansion and it's the biggest house in town. I knew Fussel lived there with his daddy, but I had never been in the place. Just driving by it gave me the creeps. Now I was parking in front of it for an official visit. Puddin sensing my discomfort said,

"You don't have to come in if you don't want to."

"No, I'll go."

We got out of the car and began walking toward the funeral home a two story antebellum mansion. Its face --- a balcony for a nose and two beveled glassed doors for a mouth --- framed in Gothic columns reeked with old southern charm. Droopy eyes of fluffy lace curtains covered the windows. We entered the house into a world of kaleidoscope colors from the oriental carpets sprawled out on the foyer's black marble floor sparkling in the light from the crystal glass chandelier hanging overhead. Walls, covered in purple and gold colored floral wall paper, hollered at me as we walked through the parlor. Palms in brass pots were scattered about the room amongst marble topped tables holding multicolored Tiffany style lamps. Two clocks sat on the white marble mantel over the fireplace. Their pendulums and brass works visible through the clear glass domes covering them. A spiral staircase led up from the parlor to the Elderidge's quarters upstairs. It was blocked by a brass plate engraved "PRIVATE" hanging from a purple ribbon across the stairs entrance. Overwhelmed by all this grandeur, I had forgotten our mission until I saw Puddin's face reflecting in the mirror on the parlor wall.

It looked as if she just learned there's no Santa Clause and it reminded me why we had come here. It was to visit the dead Grandmother wherever she may be as I saw no caskets in the room.

"Follow me," said Puddin, "a Mathas is always in the gold room."

I followed her past several doors each a different color--- blue, red, yellow and gold. We entered a bedroom through a gold door. There laid the dead Grandmother propped up on gold colored pillows in a gold gilded four poster canopy bed. An open Bible lay across her chest. The light from a reading lamp attached to the headboard fell softly on her closed eyes. If I had not known her eyes were eternally closed by death, I would have thought she had just fallen asleep while reading the Bible. Puddin bowed gracefully over her grandmother's body and kissed her forehead. I watched her lips move to the dead woman's ear and heard her whisper, "Good night Grandmother have a good rest."

After meeting Vivian and the gold room visit, I began to think Haynesville a strange place. I also thought it strange that neither her mother nor daddy had come back to the house that evening. Exhausted, I went to bed wondering what the funeral ceremony would be like in the morning. I just dosed off when I heard someone's voice calling my name and felt them shaking my arm. The voice sounded hollow and echoed like it was coming from the bottom of a well. At first, I thought it was a dream and paid it no attention. But the voice got louder and louder.

"Wake up. WAKE UP!"

I opened my eyes to see a face hovering over me. Its features hidden in the darkness. Then I heard the bedside table lamp turn on with a click illuminating the face. It was Vivian's. Without her false eyelashes, her eyes no longer assaulted me. Instead, they pleaded to me as she spoke.

"Buck's sick. You gotta help him."

"What?" I answered confused by her words.

"Please get up. Buck needs you."

"Needs me for what? Where is he? What's wrong with him?"

"Don't worry. I'll drive you there and tell you about it on the way."

That night Vivian, without saying a word, drove me to a two story broken down house located in the ally behind the Rainbow Inn. Yellow paint had peeled off its clapboard siding in splotches exposing the bare weathered wood underneath it. Wadded up rags plugged gaping holes in its broken window panes. A truck was parked in an odd position along side the street in front of the house.

Its front wheels, entangled in a hedge, were on the sidewalk. It was Mr. Mathas's truck. Even in the dark, the Mathas Bros. Warehouse Sign was clearly visible on its doors.

"Buck's having a sinking spell," Vivian explained in a calm voice like the spell happens every day.

"Sinking spell. What's that?" I asked.

"A bad one too." She said paying no attention to my question and kept on talking. "I reckon it's his mother's death that brought it on. Please, you gotta go up there and help him. I don't want anybody to know about it."

Vivian had given the order and I had no choice but to carry it out. Like a brave soldier going into battle, I marched through a pile of rancid garbage cans filled with empty beer cans and liquor bottles up the steps and BANGED on the front door with my fist. This was no time to be shy. I was running for the goal line with Vivian watching from the stands. Do it, I'm a hero. Fumble, I'm nothing. I was about to wham the door again when it opened. There stood a woman in black lace underwear. Her panties pushed down by sagging belly fat. A closer look revealed stringy bleach blond hair and deep wrinkles about her mouth and eyes. I had seen her kind at the Rainbow Inn. Hard core whores who lived by their bodies.

"Uh, excuse me. I've got the wrong place," I stammered never dreaming Mr. Mathas would be with such a woman.

"THANK GOD ALL MIGHTY! You've come," she howled. "He needs a doctor. That hard dick son of a bitch went limp on me an hour ago. He's plum out of his head or dead. He's back here on the bed. Come I'll show you."

It was an ugly sight. Mr. Mathas, clutching a half empty whiskey bottle, lay flat on his back nude on the bed. Swollen lids had replaced his eyes. Slobber dripped out of the corner of his mouth onto the bed sheet and his thighs were spread apart. The slime on his wasted penis glistened in the light from a bare bulb hanging from the ceiling. It was obvious, The Peach King of Orchard County had been up to no good.

"Ain't you gonna check him?"

"Yeah." I reached for his wrist to feel his pulse and knocked the whisky bottle out of his hand. It fell onto the bare wooden floor without breaking. Even in his alcoholic stupor, Mr. Mathas had a farmer's pulse strong and steady. I began to find this situation rather amusing and couldn't resist teasing this woman about his predicament. So I said,

"He's dead. Heart attack most likely."

My words caused her eyes to roll back so far in her head nothing but the whites showed. Her lungs grabbed all the air they could hold as she prepared to scream.

"AIN'T TRUE. DAMN IT. IT AIN'T TRUE!"

"Calm down," I said and started laughing. We don't want anyone coming in here discovering you done screwed Mr. Mathas to death."

"Buck's not dead is he? You bastard. Why'd you scare me like that? You ain't a doctor are you? Look at you. Too young to be a doctor. Vivian said she would send a doctor. Who are you?"

"Sorry, it was a joke," I said ignoring her question. "Seeing the mighty Peach King like this just seemed funny that's all. I must admit it was a bad one. Come on help me get him down the steps. His mother's funeral's in the morning. We've gotta get him back to the house. Mrs. Mathas is waiting in the car."

"Yeah, I know all about his mother bellyin' up. But he stays put. Ain't no way we're gonna get that lard belly down them steps."

"Then you'll have to stay and watch him till he wakes up," I told her. "We can't leave him alone in this condition."

"Do I look like a nurse? I screw him not nurse him."

"Well," I said laughing, "looks like you've done a good job on him."

"Buck's your party doll now," she said. "I'm getting outta here."

I had been helpless to do anything but watch the skimpy red dress slide over her head.

"You gotta help me," I insisted.

"No way sport," she said scooting her feet into a pair of white satin spiked heels and snatching a pearl studded white handbag off the table. "I'm out the door. Bye."

Her foot steps fluttered down the wooden stairs like the roll from drumsticks on a drum and she disappeared into the darkness. I looked for Vivian's car, but it was gone. Somehow I had to get Mr. Mathas to his mother's funeral in the morning. I had no choice, but to stay with him. So I sat down in the chair beside the bed and pulled the tattered bedspread over his naked body. I must've fallen asleep, for the next morning I awoke to find his nude body gone and see him step out of the bathroom wearing his customary bib-jeans and a flannel shirt. Seeing I was awake, he muttered,

"I've been trying to figure out who you are boy. I go to sleep with Lovie and wake up with you. It's like the bullfrog prince story backwards if you know what I mean."

His transformation had stunned me to the core.

He had recovered from his drunken stupor and was speaking clearly and it became obvious he was expecting me to do the same. I was afraid he would recognize me as the one alone in the truck with his daughter, but he didn't. Seeing he wasn't mad, I sternly introduced myself and quickly tried to explain why I was here.

"My name's Poon Rutherford. I brought Puddin home for the funeral. We're in school together. She wanted to take the bus, but I thought it best if I drove her home cause she was so upset."

"Mighty nice of you boy. You did the right thing bringing my sugar baby home. And I want you to know I appreciate it. But **Damn!**. Why in Heaven's name are you in Lovie's apartment?" I ain't never been so confused. Why are you here?"

Confronted with his blunt question, I decided to tell the truth and hoped he would understand.

"Uh, uh, uh," I stuttered scared to speak about last night.

"Go on spit it out. Let's hear it."

"Uh, your wife was worried about you being sick."

"She sent you here to get me. Is that it?"

"Yes sir. And when I found you passed out on the bed I thought it best to stay here till you were alright."

"My God she's right doncha know. After all these years, that woman's still looking after me. Best get moving. There's a funeral to go to," he said it like it was a football game we were going to. His cold words surprised me for it wasn't just any funeral. It was his mother's funeral. "Tell me boy. What'd you do with Lovie?"

"Nothing. She left when your wife brought me here.."

"Uh huh, that'd be her alright."

Nothing more was ever said about this situation and on our way back to the house I told him how sorry I was about his mother's death. It was then I discovered he was a very sensitive man with deep feelings for his mother. He'd been nothing like the mad man I had seen in the orchard and I listened as he talked about his mother.

"Mama had a good life. Better than most. It all started when my daddy won her at a horseshoe pitching contest up there on the square some forty odd years ago so they say. Don't get me wrong. It's not like it sounds. He didn't actually win her. It was a church social and he won her six layer chocolate cream cake. And she went with it. Nature took its course and Daddy up and married her without a dime in his pocket."

I couldn't believe it. I just met Mr. Mathas ---The Peach King of Orchard County ---in his mistress's house and now we're riding in his truck talking about his mother. I couldn't help thinking how neither he nor his wife had turned out to be anything like I expected.

"Ain't no Rutherfords around here. Where are you from boy?"

"Jonesboro, my daddy's in construction working on that new highway I-75."

"Is that so? I-75's gonna change a lot of things around here. Gonna ruin Haynesville. None of us know what to do about it either."

"How's that?"

"Won't nobody be coming here. Them snowbirds will wiz on by Haynesville on I-75 like the town was never here."

"I wouldn't worry about that. Dad says it'll be years before I-75 is completed through Georgia."

"Could be. I just hope I don't live to see it."

I thought his mother's funeral odd. But then he was The Peach King of Orchard County so it would not have been unusual for his mother's funeral to draw a big crowd of mourners. Faceless people dressed in their best sunday go to meeting clothes blended together in one big crowd to trample the St. Augustine grass in the church yard. Cars had parked bumper to bumper in long lines on both sides of Wayside Street. I thought they came to pay their respects to Grandma Mathas, but nothing was further from the truth. They had come to see Mr. Cleve Elderidge's funeral circus.

A spectacle destined to help rescue Haynesville's economy from the future evils of I-75. The funeral began by Vivian, Puddin and I following Mr. Mathas across the street to The Haynesville Baptist Church where we entered through the front door into the sanctuary. A place transformed into a tropical garden for this occasion. The heavy scent from wreaths made of orchids, roses and magnolia blossoms filled the air with a glorious sweet aroma. Gold colored tuxedo clad ushers greeted us and led us down the aisle between pews gilded gold for the funeral. My feet sank deep into the lush purple carpet with each step I took down the aisle to our seats in the front row pew reserved for us. Multiple huge gold colored ribbons, bearing the words "Rest in Peace", hung from the ceiling. They hung so low we had to brush them aside to get to our seats. Immediately, I was confronted by the silhouette of the dead woman's face on display in the coffin afloat on a floral wreath sea in front of us. A white carnation blanket hid the coffin's lower half from view. The dead woman's eyes were closed as if asleep and the open Bible still laid across her chest. Rev. Boswell stood in the pulpit listening to choirs on both sides of him humming softly a hymn while a multicolored water fountain synchronized to their humming danced in the Baptismal pool behind him. His silk golden robe made him look like an angel and the choir's golden robes made them look like a band of angels. Vivian smiled, pleased at what Cleve had done for this ceremony while Mr. Mathas rocked back and forth in the pew like he was sitting on a bed of hot ashes. Puddin sat motionless beside me staring down at the carnation pedals that had fallen off the coffin onto the floor. I heard no sobbing and felt no grief from the people surrounding me. Instead, those in attendance seemed to enjoy this spectacle.

Then an usher came to our pew and led us out the front door to a limousine just before the ceremony ended. Its chauffeur helped Mr. and Mrs. Mathas into the back seat while Puddin and I got into the front seat. We waited for the ceremony to end. Then car doors began slamming shut all around us and cars started lining up behind us with their headlights on and funeral signs in their windshields. Six pallbearers carried the coffin out of the church. Its carnation blanket swayed back and forth in rhythm with their marching feet. It soon slipped out of sight into the back of the long black Cadillac hearse in front of us. Aman in a gray Confederate General's uniform trimmed in yellow came goose stepping by our limousine. A sight that caused me to twist in my seat towards Puddin and ask,

"Who's that?"

"Sheriff Tate," she answered.

His every detail had been perfect: knee length gray coat, brass buttons, black polished boots, and a sword swinging by his side from his Sam Brown Belt. Only his mirror front sunglasses and a chrome plated whistle clinched between his teeth had betrayed his real identity. . . a small town cop. He passed so close to us that I could see our limousine's reflection pass across his sunglasses.

"Why's he dressed like that?" I asked Puddin.

"It's his funeral uniform," she replied.

He clicked his heels together in military fashion did an about face and mounted a motorcycle in front of the procession. He drew his shiny steel sword and pointed it toward the horizon and with a piercing blast from his whistle gave the order to march forward. The whistle's sound was so shrill it hurt my ears.

The funeral procession followed him snaking its way out of town and onto a sandy road going into the Mathas' peach orchards where it stopped beside a canvas tent. Here chairs had been lined up by the grave side for the immediate family and friends. Mr. Mathas knelt beside his mother's coffin and watched it descend into the rectangular hole surrounded by freshly dug earth. He plunged his hands into the dirt and sprinkled it on the carnation blanket covering the coffin while Rev. Boswell muttered, "ashes to ashes and dust to dust."

The ceremony ended and no sooner had folks turned their backs on the grave site when there appeared a lone man carrying a shovel walking toward the grave site. Soon you could hear the raspy sound from a shovel scraping the dirt down into the hole and landing on the coffin with a thud. A sight so chilling I walked away from it and stood behind a peach tree where I found comfort.

Then I noticed there were no tombstones or grave markers anywhere in the orchard. I just attended a funeral so I knew there had to be dead people buried here.

"POON!" someone yelled my name. I looked to see who it was and saw George and Fussel standing behind the hearse. Their arms spinning like propellors motioning me to come join them.

"Man are we glad to see you," said Fussel all wide eyed and bouncing up and down on the ground like a basketball as he spoke in a rapid fire excited voice. "You ain't gonna believe what we've seen."

"Yeah, we got lots to tell you. What are you doing here at this funeral.?" George asked in a voice much calmer than Fussel's. "Thought you'd be in school by now."

"I am. I brought Puddin home for her grandmother's funeral.

"Her funeral was great wasn't it?" asked Fussel. He'd given me no time to answer and kept on talking. "Daddy gets all excited about them. He can't wait for somebody to die so he can put on another big show. You ain't gonna believe what he's gonna do next."

"Yeah," George butted in, "we heard him talking about it last night in church."

"Church?. What church?" I asked, "there wasn't any church service last night because of the funeral."

"No, no you don't understand," George went on to explain, "we don't need a service to go to church. We keep our dirty magazines hidden up there in the balcony under some loose floor boards. I was feeling around for them in the dark when I heard foot steps coming down the aisle toward the altar. I looked to see who it was, but all I could see was a dim outline of that old woman lying down there with her coffin wide open. Wasn't much light to see by. Just that coming in through the church windows from the street light outside." Then George paused a moment reluctant to go on with his story.

"Yeah, yeah, go on," I insisted.

"Well," said George, " I peeked over the pew to see what was going on. What a sight. My eyes had grown used to the darkness and I could see Mrs. Mathas standing in the pulpit unbuttoning her silk blouse while Fussel's daddy sat in the front row pew watching her."

"It's true," said Fussel, "Daddy was there I saw it too. We both watched Mrs. Mathas take off her blouse and drape it over the pulpit."

"WOW! Did you see anything else?" I asked.

"Not yet," George giggled.

"Yeah," said Fussel, "we saw my daddy take off his shirt and pants while Mrs. Mathas watched him from the pulpit."

"Then we heard the rustling popping sound of nylon sliding over wool as Mrs. Mathas took off her skirt. Butt naked they both got in the Baptismal pool. 'My God,' Mrs. Mathas said happily, 'Hipsy's got the temperature just right'. Slish-slosh the churning waters in the Baptismal pool got louder and louder until Mrs. Mathas said,

'Slow down. We've got church in the morning. Hipsy will be mad if we splatter these velvet drapes with water'."

This story was so wild I thought it more their imagination than true. Besides, it sounded like something Fussel and George would make-up just to get my attention. "Yeah, then what?" I asked insisting on getting the whole story.

"Daddy started talking about how happy he would be if people started coming from all around to attend his funeral ceremonies. He said their money would help Haynesville stay like it is once I-75 opens up."

"That's the best story yawl have ever made up," I said. "Good to see you guys, but I gotta go and join Mr. and Mrs. Mathas and Puddin at the grave+side. That had been my first Haynesville funeral. I had no idea there would be more, many more.

Chapter 5

The Flint River Bridge Wreck

It's now 4 o'clock in the afternoon. The monster I-75 with its face framed by gray clouds on the horizon and green pine trees along its sides beckons us to continue our journey. Like time itself, I-75 had been unstoppable with an uncertain future and an unforgettable past. Puddin and I hated it for we knew it would eventually make Haynesville a Pennyfield. Over the years, I had watched Haynesville's people try to survive the monster's advance, but I had no idea just how desperate they had become until The Flint River Bridge wreck of 1973. Before then, I had thought all the deaths in Haynesville were accidents. But the bridge wreck brought me face to face with how far the Haynesville's people were willing to go to save their town and why the wreck had touched their heart's so deeply. Puddin and I had gone to Haynesville for the victim's funeral when Vivian told me the wreck's gruesome details. I can still hear her talking about it through her tears.

"Cleve said the cold river water froze the bodies like they died.

Arms, legs twisted every which-a-ways. He said he and Sheriff Tate barely got them stacked in the truck. It'd been a horrible sight," she said in a mournful voice befitting her words. Between her lips was her constant companion a lit cigarette. Its filter tip coated in ruby red lipstick. Smoke filled the air around her with a stale tobacco odor. "They pulled them out of the school bus after the football game in Lebanon Friday night. It crashed through the guard rail landed on its side in the river. The doors mired in the mud trapped them inside the bus. We all know Fussel drinks. Even more so on cold nights. He had to be drunk." She paused. Her face wrenched in pain. It wounded her to say Fussel's name. After all, he was Cleve's son who had now grown up to be Haynesville's High School bus driver. Wispy smoke oozed around her nicotine stained fingers as she spoke. "Cheerleaders --- Emma Sue, Linda, Barbara Jo --- all drowned. Whole football team's gone too. Fussel died later that night." She paused and crushed the cigarette out in an ash tray on the coffee table. Stick letters on its side spelled out "I LOVE YOU MOM". I knew Puddin had made that ash tray in Vacation Bible School at the Baptist Church. I hoped the snuffed out cigarette would end Vivian's gory details. But, it didn't. Tears filled her eyes and began to roll down her cheeks. She took a Kleenex off the coffee table to wipe her eyes and continued talking. "Cleve'd told me they'd tried to keep the bodies covered, but it was no use. Sheets couldn't cover bodies in those shapes. Jerry Didsbury was the last body they'd pulled from the bus. His daddy was in the boat when they found him. Cleve tried to thaw and straighten out the bodies so they'd fit in the coffins, but it was hopeless. He had to saw their arms and legs into pieces. The pieces had gotten so mixed up he didn't know which body parts went to who. So not to hurt anyone's feelings, he decided to put the pieces in closed unmarked coffins. Yawl'll see that in the morning."

I had heard enough. My parting words were simple, " I'm going to bed. See you in the morning."

I awoke the next morning to see sunbeams trickling through the window's venetian blinds bathe the bedroom in a heavenly glow. I looked out the window once again at The Haynesville Baptist Church across the street and wondered what the show would be like this time.

Mr. and Mrs. Mathas, Puddin and I sat in our reserved front row pew as usual. This morning the pew was painted black and surrounded by freshly cut orchids, roses, dahlias and magnolia blossoms. All dyed black. The smell of their sweet fragrance surrounded us like a ghostly spirit's shroud. The aisles were covered with black carpet upon which strutted black tuxedo clad ushers. Rev. Boswell sat on his throne holding a long silver shepherd's crook covered on top by a purple feather plume. He smiled at the multitude gathered before him for he knew this funeral would bring in a lot of money. Gold gilded angels wings sprouted from his back and covered the black carpet surrounding the throne. His tall miter hat, linen white robe and gold cross dangling from a gold chain around his neck made him look more like a Catholic Bishop than a Southern Baptist preacher. Choir members stood on both sides of the throne chanting in unknown tongues. There black robes were bathed in a purple spotlight glow. The multicolored water fountain, synchronized to music from a shiny-brass pipe organ, danced in the Baptismal behind Rev. Boswell. Fire and smoke shot out of the fountain every now and then. Two rows of black coffins covered in white carnations were placed before the alter.

Mr. Mathas leaned over towards Vivian and I heard him whisper," Cleve's done it. He's managed to get them twisted bodies into those coffins."

"Shoooh," Vivian shushed.

I cringed at the thought of their twisted bodies being crammed into those coffins. And thought maybe they are in those coffins and maybe they aren't.

"Psssst, pssst," Mr. Mathas whispered in my ear, "let's get outta here."

"Ok," I quickly answered.

"We're leaving," he told Vivian in a loud voice so as to be heard above all the noise and ruckus. No one noticed us leaving. Instead, all eyes were fixated on Cleve's funeral circus. As we left, I shut the door behind us hoping it would all disappear. But, it didn't. The funeral procession was beginning to line up in front of the church.

"Come on, we're gittin' my truck and gittin' outta here," Mr. Mathas commanded. "Ain't no way Cleve's gonna give them kids a decent burial."

We went out the church's front door and were immediately confronted with rows of the victims' classmates all dressed in black football and cheerleader uniforms. They stood ready to load their fallen classmates coffins into the school buses for one last ride together.

"Morning Buck," said Sheriff Tate waving his highly polished sword at him.

Mr. Mathas said nothing as we walked across the street through the ranks of the Haynesville High School marching band toward his house. I was surprised to see the band's uniforms red instead of black. As usual, Sheriff Tate was dressed in his funeral uniform which made him look like a Confederate General about to lead The British Redcoats and black school buses into battle.

"Lord what a pile of poop," mumbled Mr. Mathas. I can't believe how people come from all around and buy tickets to his funeral shows. Least he's got them gawking visitors' cars parked off the street. Put them over younder behind the church I reckon. Let's get in my truck and make this whole thing a bad memory. Mr. Mathas calmed down once he started driving the truck and began watching Sheriff Tate's funeral parade disappear in the truck's dust. But he went on complaining about the funeral. "I know Cleve and Tate mean nothing, but damn if they aren't hard to figure out at times."

"Sure create a stir," I added.

"Yep," he agreed. Mr. Mathas drove past his warehouse, bumped across the railroad tracks and stopped at Haynesville's only stoplight. It turned green and he turned left onto 41 Hwy.

"Gonna show you my brand new pasture. You're gonna meet

Leafy too." After a mile, we turned right onto a dirt road going straight west through alfalfa fields. "Leafy knows cows better than anybody. Vets come from miles around to get his help on sick critters. I built him that house younder." He said pointing toward the sunlight reflecting off a tin roof in the distance. As we got closer, I could see a house standing naked in the pasture without shade trees.

"Yep, put him right here in the pasture so he could watch over my cows."

The truck rattled on down the road spewing dust in its wake. The number of cows got thicker and thicker as we approached the house.

"Vivian's been giving me these here cows for Christmas, birthdays, anniversaries long as we've been married. Got a heep of them now. That's why I had to buy all this new pasture. Had to put Leafy out here to tend to them too. Leafy's named them all. He ran out of names a while back. Had to go to the Bible for more."

"You've gotta be kidding."

"Naws I ain't. That bull yonder is Leviticus. Leafy'll call him and he'll come running like a dog."

Our journey ended in front of two granite stone steps leading up to a three cushioned sofa placed on the front porch. Foul weather had marked its upholstery with dull yellow stains and a rotten spot where a wire spring had poked through the surface. The truck's dust cloud gave it further insult. The house was completely engulfed in cows some standing; some lying down. All chewing on something.

"Morning," shouted Mr. Mathas. "Anybody here?"

"Lordy mercy," a voice answered from around the side of the house. It sounded rich and mellow like an opera singer's baritone voice and had come from a man dressed in a sheep-skin corduroy coat. Hairy warts covered his nose and a solid white right eye wondered off to the right made his face so ugly I dared not to look at it for long. He waved his right hand in the air and I thought he was waving at us, but he wasn't. He was scattering seeds to a small peacock flock following at his heels. Their eye-like spotted feathers folded into long tails. The man's left hand was fixed and withered and his left foot etched a wavy line on the ground as he drug it through the dirt when he walked. It was obvious he had a stroke.

"Morning Mr. Buck," he said. "How are yuh? Is the funeral over? Sho-nuff sorry about them a drownin'. Real sad. Yassah, real sad. I's didn't hear yawl comin'. I's ah feedin' these birds. They'd done took to this cold weather better than I thought they would."

This ugly old man was a real talker. Mr. Mathas had to shove his words aside to introduce me.

"Leafy this is Dr. Rutherford. Dr. Rutherford this here is Leafy." Mr. Mathas said blunt and straight to the point. "We done had enough funeral for today. Thought you might show him around the pastures and all."

"Sho-nuff," Leafy said showing his gums in a toothless smile.

"All right," said Mr. Mathas," I'll wait on the porch till yawl get back. Got any Old Dog Bourbon?"

"Yassah, you know old Leafy does. Be ah chillin' in the frigidare."

Leafy wasted no time saddling up the truck. He grabbed the steering wheel with his good hand and off we went into the pastures. A withered hand and paralyzed leg hadn't slowed him down a bit.

"Looks like Mr. Buck's taken a shine to yuh. That's a heap good. How's Miz Puddin? Is she takin' the funeral alright?"

"Oh yeah," I answered. We drove over plowed fields, dead corn stalks and dried cow dung piles until we came to a big barn painted red.

"Mr. Buck sho-nuff loves them cows. He calls this place the cow hotel. It's heated, runnin' water and all. Wanna see it?"

"No, I wanna see the land."

"It's ah heap to see. Takes a spell to see it. I'll show you the pond. I likes it. Ain't it a sight?" Leafy asked after driving over a small grassy knoll. The pond was actually a three acre lake surrounded by weeping willow trees.

"Come spring, cows be ah standin' knee deep in water all through younder ta cool from the sun." said Leafy.

I pictured it alright. Cows grazing on hay in the pasture and drinking the lake's cool water on a hot summer's day. Only in my picture all the pastures, cows and lake were mine. All mine.

Then, I noticed Leafy had gotten quiet for a while and I looked over to see his head bowed. I thought him in prayer. His hand rubbing his knee nervously had told me different. He was in pain.

"Gotta tells you somethin'," he said. His eyes darted back-and-forth from his lap to the lake. "A powerful secret. It's ah bothering' me. I's gotta shed it."

"My God, what is it?" I asked.

Leafy began squeezing the steering wheel so tight his knuckles turned white.

"I's can't tells Mr. Buck. Can't tell Miz Puddin either. Nawsah wouldn't be right. I's ah need your help. So I's tells you. I's ah trusting you to be shut mouth about dis."

"I promise. I won't say anything to anybody. So, what is it you wanna tell me?"

"I's ah workin' in the church for Hipsy cauce he's laId up sick that night when I sees them."

"See who?"

"No 'count Mr. Cleve matin' up with Miz. Buck. They were ah wallerin' in the Baptismal pool like hogs they was."

"What? Are you sure?"

"Yassah, old Leafy sees good. Hears good too. They's ah talkin' about Sheriff Tate fixin' the bridge so's ta wreck the school bus."

"Damn, when was that?"

"Narin two weeks before the wreck."

"Why didn't you tell anybody. You could've saved their lives. Hipsy must've known about it too. Why didn't he say something?"

"Hipsy's born with a caul on his head. Made him deaf and blind. Some think he's half crazy. But he ain't. Don't matter. He ain't gonna tell nobody nothing. Nobody would believe him if he did. Reckon that's why Mr. Cleve and Miz Buck won't let nobody but Hipsy work in the church cause he can't hear or see nothing."

"What about you? You're Mr. Mathas' friend. He trusts you. Why didn't you tell him?"

"I know'd I could've saved them kids. I'm a heap guilty about that. But I know'd it'd hurt Mr. Buck if I told him about Miz Buck being with Mr. Cleve. You gotta help old Leafy stop these killings. There's gonna be a heep more if you don't. I's helpless."

Leafy was right. He was helpless because I hadn't believed him either. Who would believe such a crazy story from an ugly old cripple living in a cow pasture with a flock of peacocks. I thought him demented. But he wasn't.

Chapter 6

All The Motels Died

It's five o'clock when I notice our car's gas gauge is on empty. "We've gotta stop for gas," I tell Puddin.

"Ok, but hurry. You know I wanna get to Haynesville before dark."

"Traffic's mighty heavy. Looks like all the snowbirds are migrating to Florida at one time. We might not make it before dark."

We take exit 65 off I-75 and drive into a gas station and stop behind a line of gas hungry cars. Patiently I wait for the line to get shorter and shorter until we finally park beside a gas pump. While waiting for the attendant to fill the tank, I find it hard to imagine how all the traffic on I-75 had once passed through Georgia on a simple two lane Hwy going to Florida. Some had come from as far away as Sault Ste. Marie, Michigan. A trip that had to be over two thousand miles. Small town speed limits and speed traps must've made the trip take days and days. It's easy to see why in 1968-1977 snowbirds began to abandon 41 Hwy for I-75. I'm sure they had no idea what effect this would have on the small towns along 41 Hwy. The desolation was as if General Sherman had marched through Georgia again. In Haynesville, it all began that summer when all twelve rooms of the Hughes Motel were ablaze. A crowd stood watching the flames of billowing black smoke and red-yellow sparks shooting up into the night's moonless sky. Haynesville's fire truck with its siren whaling rushed to the burning rooms. In a frenzy, Billy Ray grabbed a hose off the fire truck and pointed its nozzle at the fire.

"Let her blow," he shouted to Homer who was standing by the fire truck. The flabby fire hose stiffened and Billy Ray struggled against its gyrating convulsing motions. Water spewed into the burning rooms causing the fire to sizzle and pop as the motel burned to the ground.

A week later the Glady's motel and restaurant mysteriously burned down. The Hughes and Glady families, in desperation, had really burned them down for the fire insurance money. They had left town months ago and no one was left to rebuild their motels. So their ugly charred remains were left standing alongside the highway.

The Blue Bird Motel was the last to burn. Sheriff Tate must've heard a voice announce it over the phone, "The Blue Bird Motel's on fire." There was nothing he could do. Without saying a word, I'm sure he just hung up the phone and sat alone in his office playing solitaire while it burned to ashes. There'd been no response. No volunteer fireman came to its rescue and no one watched it burn to the ground. Madam perished in the fire and her death was recorded as an accident. Rev. Boswell announced in church that sunday how proud he was to accept her insurance money as a donation.

I knew there was no way Madam's death was an accident. She would never burn down her motel for insurance money. She had money. Her livelihood never came from the snowbirds. No snowbird would have ever tolerated her one key fits all rooms security system. And none would have stayed in rooms lit by twenty watt light bulbs with no bedspreads on the beds and dingy yellow stained sheets that were seldom washed no matter how many people slept on them. Instead, her money came from the Haynesville people's sins. I saw that the summer I sold peaches in Haynesville. I saw them pair off in the rooms after the Rainbow Inn closed for the night. Funny how Madam called the Rainbow Inn a devil's den when all his work went on right under her nose at the Bluebird Motel. So when her motel burned, it not only killed Madam, it also closed Haynesville's whorehouse forever.

Everything Mr. Mathas had told me years ago when we first met at his mother's funeral had come true. Pickers had gone on welfare and no longer picked peaches in the orchards. I-75 had bypassed Haynesville leaving nothing but riffraff in its wake. He must've become aware of Haynesville's dismal future when construction began on I-75's sixty mile long segment through Atlanta. And he tried to organize meetings at the church to plan how Haynesville would survive the bad times that he knew would lay ahead.

At first, the meetings were monthly and only a few people attended them. Then the meetings became more intense when I-75 began extending south from Atlanta bypassing small towns like Calhoun and Perry. Now it was becoming clear it was just a matter of time before Haynesville would be bypassed too. Puddin and I had attended some of these meeting when we visited her parents and had heard the panic in the people's voices. I guess I was too wrapped up in my own life to have understood the seriousness of the situation for I gave it little attention.

Wilbur was the first to announce. "I'm selling my gas station and we're moving to Macon." There was no need to explain why, for everyone understood his reason to move. Judge Stoneridge tried to convince him to stay.

"Now Wilbur you're doing the wrong thing. Some of those snowbirds will always come through Haynesville. They'll miss our home cooking. They've been coming here so long yawl know some by name. They're still gonna need gas. I say you ought to stay." Two weeks later Wilbur put a for sale sign on his gas station and he and his family moved to Macon.

By 1974, Rev. Boswell's sermons had gotten short. The sunday morning town meetings were now crowded and more important than the church service. Mr. Mathas tried to control the meetings and convince people to stay in Haynesville, but it was no use. The town folk's money problems were getting worse and it became obvious little could be done to solve them.

"What are we going to do about the empty boarded up stores and burned down motels?" the funeral director Cleve Elderidge asked. They're attracting hitchhiking riffraff, rats and snakes. Weeds and trash are making them look awful. Hell, I've got people coming from all over Orchard County just to be buried at one of my ceremonies. I can't have people coming to a town that looks like this."

"Sheriff, can you get a detail together to clean up this mess?" Mr. Mathas asked.

"I'll need volunteers," Sheriff Tate answered. "Deputies Billy Ray and Homer are looking at jobs in Valdosta. I'm sure they'll leave soon. I can't arrest anybody hanging around those empty stores. Our jail only holds two. What will I do if I arrest more?"

Mr. Mathas shook his head in disgust for he had no answer to that question.

"What about our sign?" Mr. Pithum asked.

A sign's no good. Nobody's gonna drive 28 miles off I-75 to come here," Mr. Mathas answered.

"I DON'T CARE WHAT YOU THINK!" Mr. Stockman shouted, **"WE NEED A SIGN DIRECTING PEOPLE TO HAYNESVILLE!"**

"HE'S RIGHT!" Everyone shouted in agreement.

"Ok, ok, I'll look into it," said Mr. Mathas.

A ping sound comes from the gas pump bringing me back to the present. I pay the attendant and drive off blending in with the traffic going south on I-75.

Chapter 7

My Land Is Yours

The passing years had been kind to Vivian, but by 1974 Haynesville's problems had begun to show on Mr. Mathas. No longer was he the robust farmer who had chased me from the orchards years ago. His cheeks had become sunken and his once weathered tanned skin had turned pale. We got to be good friends over the years and, although he clenched a cane in his hand, he still walked in his beloved orchards. And I had been glad to oblige his company. His frail body would sway in the wind causing him to stop and lean on the cane to stabilize his wobbly legs.

"Freestones be coming in yonder," he told me shrugging his head east where peach tree rows extended to the horizon. "Roberta peaches over yonder," he said shrugging his head west. "Most pickers done gone on welfare. Most of them peaches gonna rot. I-75 is killing us. Ain't gonna be nothing left around here but riffraff. But the land's gotta prosper no matter what. It's gotta happen to keep

Haynesville alive. My daddy did it and his daddy before him. Hear what I'm saying?" he asked inching closer to me so I would be sure to hear his words.

"Yeah I do," I answered. He'd made it obvious I was to be the next generation to make the land prosper. I always wanted to inherit the Mathas Orchards, but had no idea it would come at such a high price. Growing peaches was an art I never learned. However, I knew if my inheritance was to be worth anything I had to learn to grow them as he and his ancestors had done generation after generation.

"Leafy will help you," he said. "He loves this land like I do. You'd best see him while you're here. He's been asking about you."

"I'll go tonight."

"Good, Leafy's dependable and honest as God almighty. He'll make you a good friend."

It was weird going to Leafy's house that night. I arrived around seven o'clock and found all the lights out and there were no cows standing around the house. Only an occasional frog croaking and a lone mule chomping grass beside the porch had broken the silence. I knocked on the door to see if Leafy was home. The door squeaked open and I heard a weak voice whisper, "come in." I looked through the doorway and saw nothing but darkness.

"Leafy is that you?"

"Yassah."

"Why don't you turn on the lights? I can't see a damn thing."

"Gotta be secret," he whispered.

"About what?"

"Come in. I's tells you."

I pushed the heavy wooden front door open and entered the dark living room. I shuffled my feet to feel my way around the bare floor. I could see nothing or no one.

"Where are you?" I asked for his form eluded me in the darkness.

"I's here sittin' in a chair."

I felt my way over to where I heard the sound of Leafy's voice. My fingers passed over two straight back chairs and a coat rack.

"Leafy this is crazy. What's going on?"

"Sit down and I's tells you."

"Sit where? I can't see a thing."

Then I felt Leafy grab my arm and pull me to a chair where I felt its cane bottom and sat down. I heard him swallow a few times before he said, "lets me get some tobaccy." Suddenly, a flame flashed in front of his face and burning pipe tobacco smoke filled my nose. Leafy began rattling off words between puffs. "Hipsy's laid up drunk. I worked for him in the church the other night. He swallowed a few more times and his pipe glowed each time he suck the smoke into his mouth. "Dr. Poon you gotta help old Leafy. Things ah getting worse around here. It's driving Mr. Buck feeble too. He starts ah shaking all over when he's talking about Cleve. Says he's done gone foaming at the mouth mad dog **MAD**! Talking about getting circus animals for his next funeral ceremony. Says, with all the motels burned down, he's ah wanting to rent out coffins for people to sleep in when they come to his funeral ceremonies."

"Sounds horrible. How do you know about all this stuff?"

"Listen, I's tells you. I's ah working for Hipsy cleaning the Baptismal tub the other night when peoples come in the church. I's flat on the bottom of the tub to hide. I's hears Miz. Buck ah talking, funeral man Mr. Cleve ah talking, Judge ah talking. Other folks ah talking I never heard before."

"Talking about what? You're not gonna tell me again they're still planning to kill people are you?"

"Yassah I's is. Remember last time I told you Mr. Cleve and Miz. Buck were gonna wreck the school bus and kill all them kids.

"Yeah."

"Well, they're gonna burn the whole church down now and kill everybody in it too. Mr. Cleve's saying he ah needing bodies. Miz. Buck's ah saying she needs more money to run the town. She's gotta give money to Mr. Childers to keep his drug store open. Everybody be needing money if the town is gonna stay like it was before I-75 opened. We gotta stop them. They done killed the Didsbury brothers, Earlene and Lord knows who else while yawl been in Jonesboro. Mr. Cleve's ah having them big fancy funerals all the time now."

"Damn Leafy if what you're saying is true, it makes them all cold blooded killers. You're scaring the Hell out of me now. I've gotta calm down and figure this out. Did anybody see you in church the other night?"

"I's too scared to know. You gotta help ol' Leafy. I knows they're gonna kill me. I just knows it. That's why I'm sitting here in the dark to hide cause I's hard to see in the dark."

"They're not gonna kill you. From what you've told me they only kill folks with life insurance. You ain't got any have you? Rufus didn't sell you any did he?"

"Nawsah, but I's a body and that's what Mr. Cleve wants is bodies so's to have something to bury for his big funerals."

"Damn Leafy, I'm beginning to believe you now. You're right. We've gotta do something. We've gotta go to the police, the FBI or somebody and fast."

I sat there in the dark while names and titles spun around in my brain like fruit on a one-arm-bandit: Rufus, Vivian, Rev. Boswell, banker Speckman, Sheriff Tate, Judge Stoneridge. None had come up a winner. They all had to be in on these hideous murders for their scheme to work. Leafy was right he had no one but me to go to. And I had no one but Mr. Mathas to go to for help. He was the only one left with the power to stop these murders and help bring this band of cut throats to justice. Too bad he had now grown feeble and depended on Vivian for his daily care. Down deep inside I knew there was nothing I could do either.

"Leafy, maybe we had best stay out of this mess. If they get wind we are trying to expose their scheme, they'll kill us."

"Nawsah, we ain't gonna get in it with nobody. I's an idy. All you does is go tell them insurance folks what's going on. They ought to be a heep suspicious by now anyways."

"You mean Charity Life Insurance Co. the one Rufus worked for?"

"That's right."

"That's a great idea. Like you say, I'm sure they'll be glad to hear about it and send all these cut throats to jail too." Neither Leafy nor I had any idea at that time how difficult that was going to be.

Several days later, instead of going to work in Jonesboro, I went to the insurance company in Atlanta. I had already tried to talk to Rufus and gotten nowhere. It was now time to go to the insurance company manager. The Charity Life Insurance Building in downtown Atlanta is eleven stories high. I studied the lobby index for five minutes before I discovered the Administrative offices were located in Suite 6 on the eighth floor. There I was confronted by a black young woman in a black dress sitting behind a black desk surrounded by a white shag rug. Her lips widened in a gold tooth smile and her eyes began dancing atop her half rimmed glasses when she saw me come into the waiting room. For some reason, she seemed extremely delighted to see me and stared at me a moment before she blurted out, "flibbertigibbet."

"I stood there speechless.

Then she said it again. "You know, flibbertigibbet. How do you spell it ?" She made no sense till I saw the crossword puzzle in the magazine lying on her desk. F-l-i-b-b-e-r-t-i-g-i-b-b-e-t. I spelled it for her. That caused her pencil to go pecking over the little squares in the puzzle like hens eating corn in a barn yard.

"Flibbertigibbet it fits," she said in a sight of relief. "I have been trying to spell that word all morning. Thank you so much. Oh, I'm Miss Salina, Mr. Ball's receptionist. Now, what can I do for you?"

"I would like to see the manager please?"

"We don't exactly have a manager. We have a president. I suppose that's about the same as a manager. Would you like to see him?"

"Sure, that'll be fine."

"Okay, who shall I say is calling?"

"Dr. Rutherford."

"Okay Dr. Rutherford what's the point of your visit today?"

"Just say it's very important."

"Okay," she said pushing a button on her desk's intercom.

"Ye-ye-ye-yes," a deep voice stuttered in reply.

"Mr. Ball there's a Dr. Rutherford here to see you. He says its very important."

"Sen-sen-sen-send him in."

"Okay, you may go in."

I opened the door to Mr. Ball's office to see a heavily built man a mound of stammering blubber casting a dark shadow over one end of the office. As I entered his office, his wide lips began spewing a rhythmical pulsating spray of spit mist into the air with each word he spoke. It splattered the papers lying in front of him on his desk in small dotted droplets.

"I-I-I-M-M-B-B."

Seeing him stuttering so hard to say his name, I interrupted and said, "glad to meet you Mr. Ball. I'm Dr. Rutherford. I have come to bring a serious matter to your attention."

"Wa-wa-what k-k-kind of se-ser-serious matter?"

"Murders," I answered sternly staring directly into his fat puffy eyes. My words sent his spit flying into the air again.

"W-wh-what are y-y-you talking about?"

"They're murdering people in Haynesville and calling it accidents to collect money from your insurance company. I've tried to talk to your insurance salesman Rufus about it, but he won't do anything. I'm sure he's in on it too. The whole town's in on it. So I've come to you for help."

"Wh-wh-where is Hen-hen-dersonsville?"

"No, no it's not Hendersonville. It's Haynesville.

"Th-that's a se-ser-serious ac-acc-accus charge. Wh-wh-whos been murdered?"

"There's Merietta, the football team, cheerleaders, Madam, the Didsbury brothers and more. It's been going on for years. I didn't believe it at first either. But it's true. You see one of your agents named Rufus Figly sold life insurance policies to most townspeople down there in Haynesville years ago. Now they're killing people who bought those policies and making it look like accidents so they can collect their life insurance money from your company. Check on Rufus Figly. I'm sure he's been settling up all those insurance policies so as not to raise any suspicion with your company. Your company's so big I'll bet no one's ever checked on it."

"Wh-who's co-co-mitting these mur-mur-ders?"

"My mother-in-law, funeral director Cleve Elderidge, Sheriff Tate---"Wa-wa-wait, wait," Mr. Ball interrupted me before I finished my list. "Th-tha-that's a strong all-all-alligation against the-the-them folks down th-th-there. Have yo-yo-you got p-p-proof, do-documents, f-f-finger prints, w-w-witnesses, anything?"

I thought for a moment about who would make a good witness. Not Fussel or George. They're both dead. Then there's Hipsy. Who would believe him? He is deaf and blind. It's gotta be Leafy. "Yes, I've a witness, Leafy," I answered. "He was working in the church one night and saw Cleve and Vivian drinking wine and relaxing in the Baptismal pool. That's when he heard them talking about their plan to get Sheriff Tate to wreck the bus and kill all the football team and cheerleaders. And I know Sheriff Tate did it too. Now Vivian wants to burn the church down with everybody in it."

"Wo-wo-who's Leafy?"

"He's Mr. Mathas' handy man. He lives in Haynesville right there in the cow pasture so he can look after Mr. Mathas' cows. Takes good care of them. Got them all named."

"Th-tha-that's e-e-enough. I-I-I've been in t-t-this business a lo-lo-long time and never h-h-heard anything t-t-t-this wild. G-g-got to be a j-j-joke. Y-y-you don't expect me to b-b-believe that do you?"

"IT'S TRUE! YOU GOTTA BELIEVE ME!"

"G-g-g-good bye," he said ushering me out of his office and slamming the door in my face.

"Flamboyance," Miss Saline said as I entered the waiting room. "How do you spell it?" Her eyes danced atop her half rimmed glasses as she awaited my answer.

"Oh, what the hell. It's f-l-a-m-b-o-y-a-n-c-e."

Mr. Ball hadn't believed a word I said. Then it dawned on me. I hadn't believed Leafy either. All the deaths seemed like accidents to me. It was obvious Fussel was driving the school bus drunk. Besides, The Flint River Bridge was too rickety to prevent the bus from crashing through the guard rail into the river. Surely, Merietta's death was a car accident. I almost experienced the accident myself when I looked at her wrecked car with its windshield broken and blood splattered hood. The scene was so vivid I could almost hear her scream and hear the sounds of a dull thud and crashing glass as her head went through the windshield. It was easy to imagine how the blood must've exploded from her severed neck onto the car's hood at her decapitation. And Madam, being old and feeble, could have accidentally set her motel on fire and gotten trapped in the flames. I could see why convincing Mr. Ball the accidents were really murders was not going to be easy. I had to get **proof.**

Chapter 8

The Proof

It's now 5:30 o'clock. The day has begun to chase the dusk in its quest for the darkness. I've been trapped in this car with Puddin and my past memories of Haynesville for what seems like an eternity. It sickens me. She has spoken little till now:

"You did leave food out for Flavel to feed Middleton didn't you?"

"Yeah."

"Hope that new shop is good at grooming poodles."

"He'll be fine. I wouldn't worry. Flavel will take good care of him. Besides, it won't take long to visit your mama's grave and finish her affairs. We'll be back home tomorrow."

Painted toe nails, blue ribbons around his neck and perfumed hair. Middleton is a far cry from Leafy's old blue tick hound. I ran into him when I went down to Haynesville to get Leafy's help in getting the proof. I was greeted by a dog barking inside Leafy's house. Woof-whooh whoo-woo whoof-whoooh.

"Leafy are you here?" I shouted knocking on the door.

Whoof-whoooh "Hush up Dewbaby. Hush up. I's here," he said cracking the door open just wide enough to peep outside.

A dog tried to poke its head between Leafy's legs, but his eyes remained hidden in the crotch of Leafy's bib jeans. All I could see was the dog's black nose. Whoof-whoooh Whoo, woof. "Hush up Dewbaby. This here's Dewbaby my new pup-pup. He's my watch dawg. Ain't you Dewbaby honey?"

"He's big enough to make a good watch dog," I said.

"Yassah old Leafy's ah heep scared. That's why I ah lovin' this here dawg. He's blind. But he'll sure enough tell you if anybody's around. Found him early the other morning shot in the head and sopping wet from the dew. Reckon he'd laid there all night. That's why I'm calling him Dewbaby and that's why he's blind."

I wedged myself in between Leafy, Dewbaby and the door to enter the living room. It was the first time I had seen it in the day light. The furnishings were unusual. Nothing in the room but straight back cane bottom chairs all jammed together side by side and pushed up against the walls.

"I see you got a lot of chairs. Where'd you get them?"

"At the church. Nobody wanted them so I took them."

"Chairs look stiff to me. Let's go sit out on the porch."

The front porch had been warmed by the sun from a young spring and a newborn summer. We sat there on the three cushion sofa with Dewbaby at our feet. The sofa had survived another winter and felt most comfortable. It also provided a noble throne from which Leafy could talk to his cows that would poke their heads into the porch for a nurturing pat. We talked about Mr. Ball not believing me when I told him the accidents were murders and how it seemed there was nothing I could do to stop them. I told Leafy I had to get evidence to prove it was true. The start of a drizzling rain had made our conversation even more dismal.

"What are we going to do?" I asked Leafy. "No one around here is gonna help us. Their scheme is so crazy I don't think anybody else would believe us either. It's like Mr. Ball said. We gotta prove it. No body is going to investigate anything until we get the proof. How can we get it?"

"Now, now don't fret none. I's an idy. Hipsy done told me there's a meeting tomorrow night at the church. We's gonna tape record what they're saying. We gonna record them planning murders. And that'll be the proof."

"WOW Leafy! That's a great idea. How we gonna do it?"

"I don't know yet."

"I say let's get Hipsy to record the meeting."

"Don't be silly. Hipsy can't work a tape recorder."

"Then I'll hide in the church and do it myself."

"Nawh, they'd find you for sure. Them meetings a heep secret. Lights be on in the church too. Be hard to hide.

Be just like them to poke all around in the church before the meeting starts too. They'll kill you if they find you."

Leafy was right. I thought all was lost until I saw his face light up with joy and heard him say,.

"Here's my idy. Wanna hear it?"

"Yes, yes what is it?"

"Are you a good climber?" he asked.

"Why?"

"There's a small door in the steeple that leads to the church attic. Get up there and you can record them talking real good."

"How do I get up there?"

"There's a ladder nailed by the back door. It's for climbing to the roof. Yassah, that's my idy. Hep yourself to them greens in younder. They's been soaking in pot liquor all day. Gotta be good."

We talked about his plan and decided it would work. I was to meet him behind the church after the meeting had started. The next night I waited at the Mathas's house and kept looking out the front bedroom window to see when the lights went on in the church. When the lights went on, I knew the meeting had started. So, I went across the street where I found Leafy standing under a clump of oak trees behind the church. They were the same trees Fussel, George and I stood under when we were almost struck by lightning. Leafy stuck to the tree trunk like he was glued to it. I could tell he was really scared.

"Meeting going on," I told Leafy. "There's a light in the church.

Come on show me where the ladder is."

"You know ol' Leafy can't climb no ladder and get up on the roof. I'm ah staying here behind this tree with my feet on the ground."

Wispy rain clouds had covered the moon so there was no moonlight to expose our presence. Only the light's glow from the stained glass windows could give us away now. I went behind the church and found a wooden ladder towering off the ground to the roof just like Leafy had said. Climbing the ladder to the roof was easy. However, when I got up there, all I could see was the whole length of the church's roof ridge stretching out between me and the steeple. The roof was too slick to stand on, so I straddled it like a horse and scooted across it on my butt toward the steeple. The closer I got to the steeple the more it looked like the bell was itching to ring. All it needed was a tap from my head as I crawled inside the steeple and it would ring for sure. The door in the steeple leading to the attic was there just like Leafy had said. I opened it slowly so as not to make a sound and poked my head into its uninviting darkness. I could see nothing, but I heard muffled voices like the ones you'd hear coming through a motel room wall late at night. You'd hear them, but you can't understand them. I had to get closer to understand and record what they were saying. I took my flashlight from my pocket and turned it on to see my way into the attic. It flickered light a few times and died. I thought all was lost until in the darkness I saw small squares of light shinning through a vent on the attic floor. Like a lizard stalking its pray, I slithered toward the vent on my belly and peered through its opening getting an angel's view of the sanctuary below where Vivian was standing at the pulpit. Cleve, Judge Stoneridge, Rev. Boswell, Mr. and Mrs. Pithum and Mr. Speckman were sitting in the front row pew listening to her talk. I reached in my pocket for the tape recorder but it wasn't there.

"Cleve's right," Vivian said. "We gotta kill Dr. Rutherford."

These words sent an electrical shock down my spine and knives through my brain. My heart began pounding so hard I thought its sound would interrupt their meeting. My worst nightmare had come true. They were planning my murder and I had no way to record it.

"Come on Vivian," said Rev. Boswell. "You don't mean that. Your own son-in law. Why it would break Puddin's heart."

"Don't bet on it," said Vivian. "Sometimes I think she wants to kill him too."

"Nawh," agreed Mr. Pithum"We can't kill him. Not yet anyways."

Frantically I fumbled through my pockets and felt the attic floor around me trying to find the tape recorder, but I couldn't find it. Maybe I had left it at the house or it had fallen off the roof. No matter what. I had lost it. All I could do now was listen.

"Why can't we kill him?" Vivian asked confused by their reluctance to do so.

"It'd look too suspicious," the Judge answered. "Sheriff Tate told me Dr. Rutherford's gone to the insurance company. So far they don't believe a word he said. In fact, they think he's off his rocker. Kill him now and they might think different. Might even start the insurance company snooping around here. And we sure don't want that."

"Maybe you're right," said Cleve. "We've gotta kill somebody. I haven't had a funeral in two months. I've got bills to pay. People have been coming from all around to see my funerals. Why, I could loose my reputation for having the most decorative, entertaining funerals in all of Georgia. If folks stop coming here, who's gonna pay to eat in our restaurant and buy gas at our filling station. I'm sure some would stay over night in our motel if we hadn't burned it down. What about all those flowers I've been growing in my greenhouses? You know all those out of town relatives buy them when I put their loved ones to rest in the orchards. We'll lose all that money if we don't kill somebody soon."

Unbelievable, I heard the proof and had no way to record it. Going back to find the recorder was not an option. No way was I going to leave until I heard my fate.

"Cleve pipe down," said Rev. Boswell. "We don't need more funerals around here. We've squirreled away enough money to keep this town in high cotton for quite a spell."

"Don't listen to him Cleve honey," Vivian murmured in a soft voice to console him. "We'll burn the church down just like we've planned. Kill them all. Burn them alive. That's what we'll do. Burn them all alive. There will be plenty remains for you to bury and enough insurance money to build that cathedral you've always wanted.

A BIG CATHEDRAL like the one in France," Vivian screamed before she broke down crying like a sniveling woman trying to satisfy her lover."

"Now, now Vivian," said Rev. Boswell stepping up to the pulpit and putting his arm around her. "Calm down. You know yawl ain't gonna burn the church down. There's no need for that now. Get a hold of yourself we've a serious matter here. We've gotta decide what to do with Dr. Rutherford. We can't have him running his mouth off at the insurance company."

"GET YOUR HANDS OFF ME!" said Vivian in response to Rev. Boswell attempt to console her. "You've done nothing. Your preaching's lousy. It's Cleve's funerals that draws crowds and he needs a bigger church. We gotta burn it down and get rid of that relic from the past. Sheriff Tate and I will set it on fire with jugs of gasoline. It'll be a glorious fire. Cleve will lock the doors so no one can get out."

"That's it, I've heard enough of this hogwash," declared the Judge. "Meeting's over. We'll meet again when cooler heads prevail."

Leafy had the tape recorder in his hand when I arrived back at the trees. "We done messed up something terrible," he said.

"Leafy you should've heard them. Vivian wants to kill me. It was like you said. She and Cleve want to burn the church down and kill everybody in it. I heard it all. It was like I was sitting in the pew next to all those cut-throats. They even know I've gone to Charity Life Insurance Co..

"If I had the tape recorder, we'd gotten the proof. Now we've got nothing. We can't prove a thing."

"Don't fret none," said Leafy calmly with a smug look on his face. "I's another Idy."

"You do? What is it?"

"We're gonna break into the Judge's office at the courthouse. That's what we're gonna do. Gotta be a heep of proof in there."

"Leafy you're a genius. Let's do it."

"Yassah, reckon I is."

"When are we gonna do it?"

"We gotta do it now. I's stand watch while you gets the proof. Then we're gonna haul ass."

Since they're only two street lights and one stop light in Haynesville, it was easy to walk in the shadows unseen along the sidewalk toward the courthouse. We felt safe until a car's headlights started coming toward us.

"Over here," Leafy whispered. "Get behind these bushes."

We ducked behind the thick cedar bushes in the Pithum's front yard and waited for the lights to pass us. Its black and white marking and cherry dome light confirmed our worst suspicion. Sheriff Tate was on the prowl. We laid flat on the ground and watched his car go down Wayside Street toward the funeral home.

"He's gone," Leafy whispered as he pulled a paper wad out of his bib jean's pocket. "I wanna show you something.

Hipsy's a janitor at the courthouse too. Writ this here map. Shine the flashlight on it. It shows the courthouse inside and tells us where the Judge's office is."

"WHAT! I thought you said Hipsy's blind. How's he gonna draw a map?"

"He feels everything. He feels to see what things look like. Reckon he draws it from that. Hipsy may be blind and deaf, but he ain't as dum as people think he is."

"He'd make a great witness then," I told Leafy.

"NO, no don't wanna do that. They'd kill him in a second. He's doing ah heep of good right where he is."

"How'd you know to bring that map?"

"I's full of idy's. We's gonna rob the Judge if you'd got nothing at the meeting. Well, you got nothing. So here's the map. Shine your light on it."

I took the flashlight from my pocket and aimed it at the wrinkled paper Leafy held in his hand. I tried to turn it on, but there'd been no light. In all the excitement, I forgot the flashlight didn't work.

"What's the matter? Won't it light?"

"No," I answered shaking the flashlight in the air. "Don't matter. Once I get into the courthouse, it's gotta be easy to find the office. Besides it's too late to turn back now. Did Hipsy tell you how to get in the courthouse?"

"Yep. Follow me I's shows you."

I followed Leafy around the side of the courthouse to a five foot tall window with its bottom three feet off the ground.

"Hipsy's ah keeping this window unlocked. He's a heep of help. You're gonna crawl inside. I's gonna stay here and watch for the Sheriff. If I see him coming, I'll knock on the glass with this stick. So keep ah listening."

I opened the window just wide enough for Leafy to help me slide head first through it down onto the floor inside. The hall was dark.. I couldn't see a thing. I was blind like Hipsy now. I had to let my fingers tell me what things looked like. Like a spider my fingers crawled along the wall and into a door opening. I opened the door and entered a room where my crawling fingers stumbled onto the wooden railing that led me to a large square wooden structure protruding from the floor --- the Judge's bench. The door to his private chambers had to be somewhere behind it. Again my spider like fingers began crawling over the wall searching for the door into the Judge's private chambers. I found a light switch. I wanted to turn it on and end my blindness, when suddenly my fingers felt the frame around the door leading into his chambers. Crawling on my hands and knees, I enter it and began feeling my way along a wall for a filing cabinet. I found another light switch. I sensed proof all around me. All I had to do was flick on the light switch and find it. In desperation, my trembling fingers moved toward the switch. My teeth grinding; my stomach churned so bad I was about to puke. No matter what I had to turn on the light.. One finger flick of the switch and light flashed in my eyes so bright it blinded me worse than the darkness making nothing in the room visible. Thank God his chambers were too deep in the courthouse bowels to have windows. Unfortunately, this also made it impossible to hear Leafy tapping on the glass on the outside window. As my vision gradually returned, I frantically opened the filing cabinet and began flipping through folders marked WILLS. Two Wills both signed Mr. Buck Mathas Jr. confused me. One had been dated March 1, 1955 while the other was dated April 4, 1975. A small folded piece of paper fell out of the Will's folder. It was labeled The Termination List and was signed by Vivian, Cleve, Rev. Boswell, Judge Stoneridge, Stockman and many others. There had been no time to read them all. It also had a long list of other names on it too. Again there was no time to read them all. This had to be the murder list and the proof. I had to tell Leafy. Without turning the light off or closing any doors, I ran out the Judge's chambers, through the courtroom and down the hall to the open window where Leafy had been standing guard. He wasn't there. I ran down Wayside Street looking for him. He was nowhere to be found. It looked as if he'd taken his truck to escape from Sheriff Tate. There was nothing left for me to do but get my car and drive to Leafy's house. Even in dark of night, the dirt road to his house was lined with cows. The only one to greet me when I arrived at the house was Dewbaby. I waited for Leafy to come home, but he never did. The sun had just begun to rise above the horizon when I noticed smoke coming from the direction of Mr. Mathas' cotton gin. Curiosity forced me to get my car and go to the fire. When I arrived, Sheriff Tate and others were standing around looking at the burned out timbers and soot black stone that had once been the cotton gin.

"Sorry about Leafy," Sheriff Tate said as I approached the gin.

"What do you mean? Sorry about Leafy?" I asked.

"He had an accident," he answered giving me a cold fish eye stare. "My guess is he was loading chicken coops on his truck when he saw the light in the sky from the fire. Knowing Leafy, he'd come a running to put it out. The wind must've shifted causing his truck and coops to catch fire. He might've survived if his boot laces hadn't tangled in the coops."

"That's a lie," I told Sheriff Tate in front of all those standing around the smoldering gin's remains. You know Leafy wouldn't be loading chicken coops in the middle of the night. You saw him at the courthouse didn't you and killed him like you've done the others?"

"Wild accusations," Sheriff Tate answered, "who's gonna believe you?"

"Where's Leafy's body?" I asked.

"What's left of it is on its way to the Orchard County Morgue. If no one claims it, it'll be incinerated with the rest of the garbage."

Sheriff Tate had been right. There'd been nothing I could do about Leafy's murder until I had proof. Leafy had helped me get the proof and paid for it with his life. I went to the Orchard County Morgue the next day and claimed Leafy's body. I buried it in the place he liked best . . . the cow pasture beside his home. Dewbaby, the peacocks, and the cows gathered around me as I dug his grave. They seemed to sense they would never see their master again as I placed his remains in their final resting place.

Hipsy's wife began feeding the peacocks daily while Dewbaby became their pet. Unfortunately, without Leafy's care, the peacocks died shortly thereafter. Dewbaby became their faithful watch dog witha head full of snarling teeth attached to a body that stood three feet off the ground. One ear torn off and both eyes a solid white blind Dewbaby was as ugly as his master had been. Nobody, not even Sheriff Tate, would ever come around Hipsy's place unless they were on friendly terms with Dewbaby.

After I buried Leafy that day, I wasted no time going to Atlanta and meeting with Mr. Ball, because I now had the proof. Miss Selina greeted me, "Good morning Dr. Rutherford. Go right in Mr. Ball has been expecting your visit."

I charged into his office and grabbed a handful of his shirt and pulled it into my face.

"Those bastards have killed Leafy," I said trying to shake him back and forth, but it was no use. This fat bolder of a man would not budge. “I swear to God I’ll get them for this. I can prove they are murdering people for their insurance money. I’ve got the proof!” I said waving the termination list back and forth in front of his face,

Mr. Ball was not offended by my actions and simply removed my trembling hands from his shirt and said, “C-ca-calm d-down Dr. Rutherford. What proof?”

“Read this,” I said slamming the termination list down on his desk. **READ THIS!**”

Like a bunch of bananas, his fingers fell over the list. His head, floating atop the fat roll around his neck, sank toward the desk as he began reading it. I paced back-and-forth in front of the desk trying to control my rage against this monstrous dung heap whose denials to help me had resulted in Leafy’s death.

“W-w-w what’s this paper titled t-t-te-termination list? It’s a strange t-t-t-ti-title isn’t it? These names. W-w-w-wo-who are they? And w-w-why are they on this l-l-li-list? I’m confused.”

“That’s the murder list,” I answered. “Look who’s signed it. The murderers that’s who. Check it out. I’ll bet you’ll find the names on that list are the ones your insurance agent Rufus Figly sold life insurance to back in the 60’s.”

“Wh-wh-what’s wrong with him s-s-se-selling insurance? That’s what he is s-s-su-pupposed to do. After all we are an insurance c-c-co-company.”

“You don’t understand,” I tried to tell Mr. Ball. Notice the names checked off the list. They match those who’ve been murdered.”

“Th-th-there’s a lot of names c-c-ch-checked off,” he said after studying the list.

“Exactly, Orchard County Morgue issues a death certificate to the next of kin. They give it to Judge Stoneridge who sends it to your company and collects hundreds of thousands of dollars on behalf of the beneficiary who gives it to the committee. Then the committee distributes the money to whoever needs it. That's how Haynesville has survived after being bypassed by I-75. As I've said, check the names on the termination list. I know they will correspond to the accidental death claims made to your insurance company."

"Co-co-committee. Wh-wh-whose on it?"

"All Haynesville's prominent citizens: Funeral director Mr. Cleve Elderidge, Judge Stoneridge, Rev. Boswell, banker Mr. Speckman, town council Mr. and Mrs. Pithum, the mayor and Sheriff Tate. And it's run by Vivian, my wife's mother."

"S-s-stop. Y-y-you're painting a w-w-w eird picture. I-l-l've looked into Haynesville's insurance c-c-claims since t-t-the last t-t-time you were h-h-here and I admit they're c-c-c-curious. There's b-b-been nineteen accidental d-d-deaths r-r-re-reported since 1966 w-w-with payments over a-a-a-million d-dollars going to a Judge S-S-Stoneridge on behalf of The H-h-ha-Haynesville B-B-Baptist Church."

"That's what I've been trying to tell you."

Yea-yea-yeah, but it doesn't p-p-prove anyth ing. That's b-b-be-been over a period of ten years. It c-c-co-could happen. B-b-besides, what are y-y-you worrying about, y-y-your name's not on t-t-the list."

"Don't matter. They're gonna kill me because they know I'm coming here. I've even heard them planning to murder me."

"Je-Je-Jesus. Y-you better g-g-go to the p-p-po-police."

"You gotta be kidding. Sheriff Tate's the police and I'm sure he's the one whose gonna kill me. He's the law in Orchard County. Nobody will do anything to stop him either. What do I have to do? Buy you a front row seat to my murder before you'll believe me?"

"Termination list is i-i-interesting, but an eye w-w-witness to these so called m-m-murders would be b-b-be-etter."

"No time for that now. We've gotta save the unchecked names on the list. And we've gotta do it now. It's just a matter of time before they're murdered."

"I-I-I-I hope not, but I can't do anything without more p-p-proof. Besides, I'm s-s-su-sure there're a lot of p-p-pe-people down there who w-w-wi-will testify that these have all been a-a-ac-accidents. You need p-p-pe-people who w-w-wi-will say they are m-m-murders. You n-n-ne-need people that h-h-ha-have seen the m-m-murders. H-h-ha-have you got any?"

I left Mr. Ball's office knowing he was right. Not everybody in Haynesville was in on the committee's deadly scheme. The committee had been so clever in making the murders look like accidents there was no need for anyone to suspect otherwise. Leafy's death had left me alone in my struggle to expose the murders. A struggle that changed drastically a few weeks later when Mr. Mathas died.

Chapter 9

THE ART IS LOST

Peach trees had been in full bloom the March of 1975 when the art of growing Mr. Mathas' delicious tree ripened "freestone" peaches was lost. That's when they found him lying on his back in the orchard with his eyes wide open staring up at the mid day sun. They'd placed his lifeless body on the manure sacks in the back of the truck and rushed him to Orchard County Hospital. Getting the news, Puddin and I had immediately driven all that day from Jonesboro to the hospital where we rushed into the lobby. The lobby was filled with rows of blue vinyl sofas sandwiched in between the gift shop and a reception desk. A maple wood coffee table covered in magazines, ashtrays and unfolded newspapers was placed in front of each sofa. Fluorescent lights flickered and hummed at us from their lofty perches in the acoustical tile ceiling. Grit on the terrazzo floor crunched under our shoes as we approached the reception desk where a lady with silver colored hair, shimmering under the fluorescent lights, was sitting. She was slumped over a quilt draped over her lap. So busy quilting, she failed to notice us come to the desk.

"Hello, we need to find a patient. Mr. Mathas where is he?" I asked. My words caused her to remove a sewing needle from between her teeth and stab it into the quilt.

"Buck's not allowed visitors," her words whistled through her ill fitting dentures, "Doctor's orders."

"He's my daddy," Puddin explained, "and I'm gonna see him. Come on Poon to Hell with this. There's intensive care. I know he's in there," she said walking into the ICU through doors marked restricted. All the beds in the ICU were filled with patients propped up on pillows and oblivious to the nurses meandering around them preparing medications and watching heart monitors. By accident. I spotted Mr. Mathas propped up in bed 3.

"He's here." I shouted.

Puddin slowly approached the figure propped up in bed. There was no familial greeting. No how's my sugar baby doing question from her daddy's twisted face.

"Daddy can you hear me?" Puddin begged. "Please squeeze my hand if you can hear me." There was no response. The stroke had made him mute. Tears filled her eyes and spilled onto her cheeks as she realized she would never hear her daddy's voice again. We'd left the hospital that night not knowing if he would live or die.

Early the next morning, with the sounds of bacon sizzling, egg shell crunching against the skillet's edge and the smell of coffee perking on the stove, we anxiously awaited word of Mr. Mathas' condition from the hospital. That is when, to my surprise, Sheriff

Tate interrupted our breakfast by knocking on the back porch screen door.

"Come in," said Vivian.

"Morning," he said bowing politely to Vivian and Puddin. "Sorry to barge in like this, but there's a meeting at the hospital and I've been asked to bring Dr. Rutherford to it."

Vivian and Puddin said nothing as I left the house with Sheriff Tate. I sensed they had already anticipated him taking me to the hospital and knew all about the meeting. We took the freight elevator from the lobby up to an unmarked floor and entered a dimly lit corridor lined with medical supply boxes stacked to the ceiling. I followed the Sheriff to the end of the corridor where we were greeted by an elderly nurse with a sterile smile standing in front of a sign marked "Toxic Waste". Her shoes were polished white and a starched white skirt flowed below her knees to the floor. A nurse's hat sat squarely on her head matching her white hair. Sheriff Tate slithered into the background while she beckoned me to follow her across a threshold into a room filled with rhythmical sounds from hissing oxygen tanks and beeping monitors. They came from Mr. Mathas' half paralyzed body as he lay in bed with his eyes half open. His twisted face flushed a blood red. Yellow tinged fluid drained from tubes in his nose and bladder. Yet, amongst this death's paraphernalia, he held a fountain pen in his right hand. Ghoul like figures had gathered around the bed. Two wore a black hood and a black robe. It was impossible to tell if they were men or women. The others hid their emotions behind fortresses of wrinkled foreheads and arched eyebrows. It became obvious. This was no ordinary meeting.

As I approached the bed, a thin gentleman with a whirlpool bald spot on his head rose in a spiral motion from his seat. His white linen suit was a sharp contrast to those around him dressed in dark funeral clothes.

"I'm Judge Stoneridge," he said extending a knobby hand in my direction. I shook it gently for fear of damaging its arthritic deformed bones. "Come Dr. Rutherford," he said. "Let me introduce you to those who've gathered here for this most sad occasion." His wispy goatee bobbed up and down like a deer's tail in flight as he spoke.

I thought his words odd for I knew him and almost everyone in the room. I had seen them over the years in town and church too. Why he was now introducing me like I'm a stranger made me feel ill at ease.

"This is Mrs. Bebe Pithum our court recorder." said the Judge as his arthritic fingers waved towards a lady dressed in a blue and white poka dotted dress. Her quivering fingers froze on the typewriter's keys when the Judge spoke her name. Her eyes, blank and empty as a desert, peered at me through a netted veil hanging off her black pillbox hat. Her red button mouth looked too small to speak. She remained silent.

"Sitting next to Bebe," the Judge said bowing to a bushy gray headed man, "is her husband and Notary Public Mr. Roy Pithum." He leaned over the bed to shake my hand causing his silk tie to dangle in Mr. Mathas' face. Mr. Pithum's beady little eyes deep set in a face pinched into a sharp pointed nose stared at me briefly. He said nothing.

"The identities of these two will remain unknown," the Judge said casting a fleeting glance toward the two hooded figures. No movement or sounds ever came from the two piles of black hoods and robes. I had no idea who they were or why they were here.

"You know Rev. Boswell," said the Judge proceeding on with his introductions.

"Yes I do. He joined Puddin and me together in the Holy Bonds of Matrimony."

Judge cleared his throat, raised his arms high in the air and introduced the last man at the bedside, "I'm proud to introduce Buck's worthy opponent the honorable banker Mr. Cecil Speckman. Through out eternity may God or the devil referee them as they battle each other in their quest to grow the most delicious Georgia Peach either in Heaven or Hell."

"Now I want you to meet our honorable mayor Mr. Andrew." Like a water-witch dousing the ground, he then lowered his quivering arms over a man who was so hunched over his eyes could only see the floor. Locks of parallel black hair were combed neatly over his balding head. He looked unable to move. So I went over to shake his hand and knelt down to look into his eyes. They were pearly white without the darkness of pupils and slithered back and forth beneath crusty eyelids.

"Glad to meet you mayor. How do you do?" I asked and to my surprise he answered in a booming bass voice.

"My prostate is big as a watermelon, but I still fart therefore I live." His comment brought a titter of laughter from the group.

"Uh," the Judge grunted. "Let's get on with the meeting. Are you ready Buck?" Mr. Mathas responded to the question by making a purposeful movement of the pen over the paper pad lying on the bed beside him. I was dumbfounded, for he was conscious and had understood every word that had been said. Mrs Pithum leaned over her typewriter and looked at the writing on the pad and announced, "Buck's written yes, your Honor."

"Fine, I'll read the Will he's written this very morning. It begins. Be it known this 15th March day, 1975. I Mr. Buck Mathas Jr. son of Mr. Buck Mathas Sr. leave two thousand dollars to my wife of forty-seven years Vivian. All these people in the room had made it hot and stuffy causing sweat to soak my shirt. My sweating was made even worse by hearing the Judge read Mr. Mathas' Will while he was still alive.. Yet anticipating what the Will might say stirred up memories from long ago when I first sowed my greedy seeds and married Puddin to get into the wealthy Mathas family. Now it's harvest time. The land is gonna be mine. I'll be rich and own most of the county.

The Judge continues reading, "Dr. Rutherford is to inherit the orchards and adjacent land on the survey recorded at The Orchard County courthouse as long as he remains faithful and married to his daughter Puddin Mathas. Be it known **should anyone prove him unfaithful** his inheritance will immediately pass to The Haynesville Baptist Church Committee. I say the Will reading's done," said the Judge. All in the room remained silent as the Judge walked over to me and forcefully began to shake his fist in my face. "I warn you Dr. Rutherford I'll protect the Will's conditions with my life. But if you violate it in any way, I'll gut you like a hog and skin you like a skunk. Am I clear?" His lips were so close to me that I could feel his spit on my face as he spoke.

His words meant nothing. They didn't scare me at all. I felt like jumping up and down on the bed and shouting THANK YOU Mr. MATHAS. So, I answered, "Yes. Yawl know I'll always love Puddin and I'll always be faithful to her too."

But the Judge hadn't finished talking and said, "there are two here whose identities will remain unknown. Their eyes will be upon you, their ears to the ground. Nothing would please me more than for you to violate the Will so we could give all your inheritance to the church committee." Having said those words, the Judge turned towards Mr. Mathas lying in bed and asked, "Buck are you ready to end this meeting?" Again Mr. Mathas moved the pen over the paper pad lying beside him on the bed and again Mrs. Pithum leaned over her typewriter to see what he had written and again she announced.

"He says yes your Honor."

"Dr. Rutherford you may leave," were the Judge's last words.

There was nothing left to do but tiptoe over to where the nurse was standing motionless at the door. Her once icy face had melted. Tears were in her eyes and she bit her lips trying not to cry. Her trembling fingers struggled to turn the knob and open the door. I paused at the door and heard the respirator's hissing stop. A woman burst into tears. They had unplugged Mr. Mathas. He was dying. As I walked down the hall, I listened to the heart monitor's beep, beep grow faint and wondered which beep would be his last. It was then that the conquering hero within me vanished taking away my contentment for life and rendering my future plans meaningless. Mr. Mathas had died.

Cleve knew Mr. Mathas was well liked in Orchard County and lots of people would buy tickets to come to his funeral. So he made it a splendid affair. In true Mathas fashion, gold was the ceremony's theme color. Gold gilded pews were placed in the church's front yard and glittered in the sunrise. They were placed there so folks could witness Rev. Boswell's arrival at the church in a black Cadillac with angels painted gold on the doors. The doors opened and two men dressed in golden robes dashed out of the car to unroll a brilliant gold carpet from the front car door to the church's door. Out stepped Rev. Boswell in a golden robe with his new found friend Sweet Daddy Grace, a Negro tent evangelist, in a black robe. It was plain to see Sweet Daddy was an albino. Pure white as the fresh fallen snow. Fluffy long white hair foamed like whipped cream around his colorless eyes and lips. Sweet Daddy faced the church and clapped his black gloved hands four times which summoned, six men clad in golden robes all playing trombones, to the church's front door. I had never heard the tune they were playing before, but its rhythm started folks to dancing. Rev. Boswell and Sweet Daddy began dancing and shuffling around on the gold carpet towards the church's front door where two men, dressed in gold robes, were kneeling and holding baskets to collect tickets. Folks formed two lines, put their tickets in the baskets and entered The Haynesville Baptist Church for Mr. Mathas' funeral ceremony. A life sized statue of Mr. Mathas had been placed in the Baptismal pool which was now filled with flashing lighted Magnolia blossoms. Cleve had added two more Baptismal pools just for this occasion. Both with fountains swishing gold colored water in the air. The choir clad in their golden robes danced in circles around the two Baptismal pools singing and banging on tambourines in rhythm with the trombones. Their song had a Doo-Wop 50's toe tapping sound which everybody loved. Cheers would go up from the crowd every now and then as the music got louder and louder.

Suddenly it all stopped when Rev. Boswell and Sweet Daddy Grace, standing behind the pulpit, raised their arms upward towards heaven. Once it was silent, they lowered their arms to the floor and Rev. Boswell asked, "does anyone have words to say about Buck?" That'd started a ho-rang about how wonderful Buck had been. As they spoke, a gold gilded coffin with purple flashing lights containing Mr. Mathas' body began to descend from the ceiling to finally take its resting place before the pulpit. Rev. Boswell ended the service with a prayer wishing Buck's soul a joyous journey to heaven.

Six pallbearers dressed in bib jeans, flannel shirts, brogan shoes and impeccable white brimmed hats came down the aisle to pick up the coffin and carry it to the front door. There was no hearse waiting to receive the casket. Instead, the pallbearers carried it across the street to his home where he was buried in the back yard. Story goes Vivian had him buried there to keep an eye on him at night. The inscription carved on the headstone proved the story true. It read:

HERE LIES THE PEACH KING
OF ORCHARD COUNTY
1921-1975
" NOW I KNOW WHERE YOU ARE AT NIGHT"

Mr. Mathas had been no Saint so I thought Vivian's antics appropriate.

After his passing, my greed had become a dead dream. For the art of growing freestone peaches and raising cows now lay in the grave with Mr. Mathas and Leafy. Leafy was a self satisfied man who never learned to read or write. He had given Mr. Mathas his heart's love and his hand's labor. When he lived, the peaches and cows were managed to perfection. The peaches were picked, culled and loaded off to market. Cows got fed hay in winter and tended to when sick. When their masters died, they grieved to death and their maggot infested bodies littered the pastures. The peach trees yielded fruit, but few picked them in LBJ's Great Society. I had always thought Leafy would be here to help me with the orchards and I did not learn the art of growing freestone peaches. All I harvested were tasteless clingstones that no one would buy.

That's when I tried to convince the town folks to electrify the orchards with an amusement park called Peach Land. Every thing in it would look like peaches. Giant peaches for ferris wheel chairs. Peaches for merry go round horses. Peaches strung one behind the other for roller coaster cars. Peaches for concession stands with stems and leaves. Peach seed shaped restrooms. Some original trees would remain giving the park a natural peach orchard feeling. There would be a hotel with balconies filled with tourist admiring pink-red peach blossoms in spring. Pickers in bright colored uniforms would gather ripe peaches in summer. Buses would shuttle tourist along the Peach Blossom Trail while guides explained how Colonel Sam Hill, after the Civil War, tried to grow seedless, fuzzless peaches. He had been successful too, but consumption killed hm and he took his discovery to the grave. Legend goes he is buried somewhere in these orchards. No one knows exactly where. Peach Land was a dream I knew would never come true.

Chapter 10

The Church Fire

Our car's engine drones on and on as we continue our drive down I-75 towards Haynesville. I-75's a boring road. Rest stops along I-75 have replaced the picturesque bustling small towns that once dotted the landscape along 41 Hwy years ago. Sure the rest stops are often a welcome sight, but do little to break-up the endless miles of dull countryside. Bored by this dull drive and Puddin's stubborn silence, my mind remains fixated on my greed. I always thought greed was like good health either you had it or you didn't. I'm so eaten up with greed that I'm often tempted not to expose the Haynesville murders for fear of loosing my inheritance. What about all those innocent murdered people? And what about those poor souls who are going to be murdered? My conscious naws at me constantly telling me I've got to keep going to The Charity Insurance Co. and I've got to keep seeing Mr. Ball until he realizes the deaths are not accidents but murders. My last visit was only a week ago. Miss Selina greeted me when I entered the office. I was surprised to see there were no chairs in the waiting room.

“Well Dr. Rutherford I see you coming to the meeting. Mr. Ball told me to have you wait. He’s not happy about you coming back here.”

Miss.Selina always wore a black dress that matched her black desk, black hair and mocha-fudge complexion. Whether it was made of wool, silk or cotton, the dress was always black. That day it was made of silk with a mid-thigh hem that slipped gracefully over her black-net stockings. The movie magazine she held in front of her face that morning announced there would be no crossword puzzle spelling bee on this visit.

“Why aren’t there any chairs in the waiting room today?” I asked.

“Mr. Ball says we don’t need any chairs. He doesn’t want anybody waiting long enough to sit down.”

“I’m waiting,” I said pacing back and forth erratically on the white shag carpet.

“Sen-sen-sen-send him in a voice stuttered over the intercom’s black speaker sitting on Miss. Selina’s desk.

“Dr. Rutherford, you may go in now.”

I entered his office and was met with a cold greeting.

“I can’t say I w-w-w-anna see you again. I-I-I’m sorry to hear about your mother-in-law’s a-a-accident. Mr-Mr-Mrs. V-V-Vivian Mat-Mat-Mathis I think her name was. Wa-wasn’t it-it?”

“Yes, that’s right.”

“H-h-horrable a-a-a-accident. I’ve r-r-r-read S-S-Sheriff T-t-t-Tate’s r-r-report.. Y-y-yes a horrible accident.”

“It wouldn’t have happened if she wasn’t trying to burn the church down,” I said. “There’s gonna be more murders in Haynesville too. And I fear for my life. I can’t believe you won’t lift a finger to do anything about them.”

It was then I noticed other people in Mr. Ball's office. I had no idea who they were.

"No-no-now, no-no-now, Dr. Rutherford, I understand your frustration. Th-th-th-th-that's why I've called this m-m-meeting." Then Mr. Ball stopped stuttering and pointed towards a uniformed law officer.His uniform was distinctly different from Sheriff Tate's. This was no small town cop. This was a real law officer.

"Th-th-th-this is Officer Cuff. He's a Georgia State Tro-Tro-Tro-Trooper. He's got jurisdiction over Orchard County."

I couldn't believe it. Mr. Ball was finally on my side. My spirits soared to the heavens. No longer was Sheriff Tate going to intimidate me. A real Georgia law officer was coming to investigate the murders. I almost could see him riding into town on a white horse.

"Si-si-sit down and te-te-tell Officer Cuff what you think is going on in Haynesville."

"Glad to meet you Officer Cuff."

"Oh, e-e-excuse me please," Mr. Ball interrupted. "This is Miss Crystal Car-Car-Car-Card our court recorder. She's gonna typ-typ-type your d-d-deposition just in case we need it for hearings and such. I tru-tru-trust that's all right with you?"

"Yes, by all means. Let's begin"

"Okay," nodded Mr. Ball, "te-te-te-tell us everything you remember about the church fire accident that killed Mrs. Mathas."

"Well, I had over-slept and gone to church late that Sunday morning."

"Uh, the time and date if you please," said Officer Cuff, "for the record you know."

Well, it was October 31st. Sunday morning this year 1976 around eleven forty. I remember because the church service was about over."

"Okay, go on," urged Officer Cuff.

"When I entered the church through the back door, I remember smelling fresh coffee brewing down stairs in the kitchen. I planned to stand in the hallway until the service was over, but the coffee aroma lured me down stairs to the kitchen. Everything was quiet. No sound was coming from the congregation. I saw why when I crept past the open doors.

The congregation had their heads bowed and eyes closed in silent prayer. I remember seeing Puddin sitting alone in the pew without her mother."

"This Puddin, that's your wife?" Officer Cuff asked.

"Yeah."

"Mrs. Mathas was your mother-in-law. Is that right?"

"Yeah, that's right."

"Proceed, I just wanna make sure everybody is identified for the record."

"I understand. Do you want all the details?" I asked.

"Kee-ee-keep going. Yo-yo-you're doing fine," Mr. Ball urged me.

"Okay, well I followed the fresh-perked coffee aroma down stairs to the kitchen. The door was closed so I reached for the door knob to open it. That's when I heard the familiar voices coming from inside the kitchen. So, I stood there listening with my hand frozen on the knob."

"Yeah, yeah," said Officer Cuff getting impatient with all my details. "Get to it. Who were they? What did they say?"

"It was Vivian, uh Mrs. Mathas. She was arguing with Sheriff Tate about burning the church down with everybody in it. She wanted him to do it, but he refused."

"What? Why that's the wildest thing I've ever heard, said Officer Cuff. Mr. Ball has told me you said Sheriff Tate's a murderer. Killing folks in Haynesville for their insurance money."

"Le-le-le-let hi-him finish," Mr. Ball interrupted. "Go on Dr. Rutherford."

"Sheriff Tate's refusal surprised me, because I knew he had murdered the others. I couldn't understand why he was refusing to cooperate with her this time until." I paused a moment.

"Until what? Until what? Officer Cuff persisted asking.

"Ple-ple-ple-please let hi-hi-him speak."

"Until I heard Sheriff Tate say his daddy was upstairs in the church. That's when I understood why he'd refused to set the church on fire. He didn't want to kill his daddy. I've told Mr. Ball all this before. Why do I have to go over it all again?"

"Go-go-go on," Mr. Ball had encouraged me. "I want Off-Off-Off- Officer Cuff to hear it too."

"Okay. Well, their voices got muttered and drowned out by the congregation singing upstairs. The organ music had gotten louder. I couldn't hear them talking anymore so I pressed my ear against the door to hear them better when . . . when ... when . . ." I paused again. I couldn't believe I had to relive this horrible scene over and over again in my mind.

"When WHAT?" Officer Cuff asked insisting I go on talking.

"That's when the door sprang open and I stumbled into the kitchen. I'm sorry," I said wiping the tears from my eyes with my hands until Mr. Ball gave me a tissue. "Even though Vivian was a hateful woman who probably deserved to die, I still found her death painful to talk about."

"Yo-yo-you wanna bre-bre-bre-break?" asked Mr. Ball.

"No, I wanna get this over with. Like I was saying, my weight caused the door to spring open. I stumbled into the kitchen and scared Vivian so bad she dropped the glass jug she was holding. It must've been filled with gasoline. When it smashed to pieces on the floor, it splattered her and the kitchen stove's open gas flame with gasoline. In a flash, fire hissed through the air. Vivian's mouth opened to scream, but there'd been no sound. Flames consumed her body and turned it into a mass of flailing arms and legs. Smoke filled the kitchen and poured into my lungs. I began choking. I heard Sheriff Tate choking and coughing too. 'Go warn the others,' he said. 'or they'll all be burned alive'. Just before I leaped through the flames and out of the burning kitchen, I looked back over my shoulder at Vivian's burning body which was now a mass of writhing flames slumping to the floor. Sheriff Tate was trying to snuff out the flames with his coat, but it was no use. With the gasoline soaked floor ablaze, it was impossible for him to get close enough to her to do any good."

"Horr-horr-horr-horr, terrible," gasped Mr. Ball.

"The smoke was so thick, it'd burned my eyes. I couldn't see Sheriff Tate, but I heard him yelling above the crackling flames of Vivian's burning body, 'Get outta here go warn the others!' Following his command, I ran up the stairs and raced through the hall into the sanctuary shouting, 'FIRE GET OUT! FIRE GET OUT FIRE!!!' The congregation and I scrambled out the front door and into the church front yard. We stood there watching the flames licking the basement windows when Sheriff Tate appeared in the front door. He was covered in soot. I alone knew it was soot from Vivian's burning body. **'IS EVERYONE OUT!!?'** he screamed. **'I THINK SO!'** Rev. Boswell screamed back. 'Get the fire truck,' ordered Sheriff Tate. The sight of smoke leaking around the stained glass windows panicked members of the congregation who wanted to run back into the burning building and get fire extinguishers to save their beloved Haynesville Baptist Church. The very church in which Vivian wanted to burn them alive. One member of the congregation tried to run through the front door into the church's burning flames, but Sheriff Tate put his leg across the door to block his entry. 'Stay back,' he'd said. 'It's too dangerous. Let it go.' I believe Sheriff Tate wanted the church to burn down and destroy all evidence of their arson and maybe that's also why the fire truck never came. I don't know."

"T-tr-tr- true we found no evi-evi-evidence of ar-ar-arson," said Mr. Ball.

"Yeah," Officer Cuff agreed. "The glass jug could've been used for cleaning fluid as far as we know. You've said it was hard to hear their voices through the closed kitchen door. How do we know if what you heard was really true?"

"Ah-ah-agree," Mr. Ball said nodding his head up and down. "S-s-s- so as far as the C-Charity Insurance Co. is concerned, Mrs. Mathas' death has been r-r-r recorded as a most unfortunate acc-acc-accident," he said in a tone that sounded like he was through with this matter. But I wasn't.

"I TELL YOU SHERIFF TATE'S KILLING PEOPLE DOWN THERE IN HAYNESVILLE!!!" I shouted over and over again. "I heard Vivian talking about burning the church down months ago. She wanted Sheriff Tate to lock the doors and trap the congregation inside so they'd all be burned alive. She wanted their deaths to look like an accident. She wanted to give Cleve bodies for his funerals and insurance money to build a bigger church."

"That's one Hell of a story for a man without any proof to back it up," said Officer Cuff. "I'm sure Sheriff Tate won't appreciate your accusations. Why I've known Buba Tate nearly all my life. He's no liar. Dr. Rutherford, you said Buba Tate uh I mean Sheriff Tate didn't wanna burn the church down. You also said he tried to save Mrs. Mathas by smothering out the flames with his coat. A heroic deed. So unless you got proof, it's his word against yours. Have you got proof?"

"No, not yet, "I answered.

"Th-th-th-that's it t-t-then. Miss Card let the record show Mrs. Mathas death was an accident and two hundred thousand dollars d-d-d- death benefit will be given to her estate executor Judge Stoneridge. I wanna t-t-t-t-thank yawl for c-c-c-coming." Officer Cuff and I left Mr. Ball's office and were greeted by Miss Selina.

"Bye gentlemen," she said glancing over the top of her movie magazine. "I trust yawl had a nice meeting."

"I need to make a phone call," said Officer Cuff, brushing Miss. Selina's comment off like she never had anything important to say.

"Certainly, right this way," she said rising to her feet accompanied by the sound of crackling electricity from her silk black skirt sliding down over her black netted silk stockings. She directed Officer Cuff into an empty office next to Mr. Ball's.

Not wanting Miss Selina's comment to go totally unnoticed, I threw back a soft dart. "The meeting wasn't all bad." When she smiled, I knew I hit the target. I wanted to escape Officer Cuff as fast a possible. So I rushed out into the hall and pushed the elevator button going down. [Bing] the elevator bell rang and [ru-rap] the doors slid open. I still could not get the sight of Vivian's death out of my mind. And the murders. How am I gonna stop them?. [Bing] the bell rang and [ru-rap] the doors closed signaling my descent down to the lobby.

Then suddenly a hissing, pssst, psssst sound came from behind my neck followed by something poking me behind my left knee. I jerked my head around to see what it was when I was confronted by two bull's eye target eyes. Round rimmed glasses framed the outside of the target while dot black pupils formed its center. The eyes had reacted to my jerky head movement by getting so wide they almost covered his entire long slender face. A face so close I could see each gray eyebrow growing out of its forehead. I looked down to see the charcoal suit he was wearing draped neatly over his coat hanger thin shoulders. It was divided down the middle by a blue and gold striped neck tie. There was a brown leather brief case, dangling from his left hand, that poked me behind my knee. He was so slick looking I immediately pictured him a Wall Street Charlie.

"Jes! You scared me," I exclaimed.

"Shoooooh," he whispered.

"What do you mean shoooh we're the only ones in here. "Who's gonna hear us? What do you want?" I asked in a whisper to this mysterious person.

"I been riding this elevator all morning waiting for you," he answered, "I wanna help you."

"With what? How?" I answered, confused about meeting this strange person in the elevator.

"With legal assistance. You really need it," he assured me. "Sheriff Tate's got you so hog-tied and bum-fuzzled you don't even know there's law outside of his jurisdiction."

"What are you talking about? How do you know about Sheriff Tate and how do you know about me? Who are you?"

"I'd rather not say at this time. Let's just say I know more than you think I do about the Haynesville murders and I can help."

[Bing ru-rap] the elevator doors open signaling our arrival at the lobby. It was clear this guy wasn't about to give me any more information and he wasn't about to give me his name either. So I stuck with the name I had given him . . .Wall Street Charlie.

"Push twelve," he said, "and we'll ride back up."

Before I could push the button, five young women rushed into the elevator. The doors closed and all of us ascended upward in our closed in little room. I knew there would be no conversation with Wall Street Charlie now. There was nothing I could do but wait for the women to get off the elevator. I thought the young women would have chattered to each other, but not a word was said. They just stood there looking professional in their feminine styled navy-blue business suits trimmed with white collars and cuffs. Shoulder length blond hair, parted in the middle, rolled down over their shoulders. Each cuddled briefcases in their arms like babies. I thought they'd never get off and I would never get to speak to Wall Street Charlie alone again. Then [bing, rue-rap] the elevator doors opened and like a darting school of fish the women were gone. Finally, Wall Street Charlie and I were alone again.

"Can't we get off this elevator and talk?" I asked.

"No. You know folks down there in Haynesville are full-moon mad at you. Who knows what they'd do if they knew I was gonna help you. I don't wanna stir up the pot until we get the goods on them. We've gotta talk here. It's private. No one will suspect us talking about the murders on this elevator." [Bing, rur-rap] the elevator doors opened on the tenth floor. No one's there. [bing-rur-rap] the doors close and we descend back down to the lobby. "If anyone gets on here, I don't want you standing next to me or talking to me," he whispered in my ear. [Bing, ru-rap] the doors opened, but no one enters the elevator. The doors closed and Wall Street Charlie said, "push twelve."

"Who are you?" I asked.

"I'm a lawyer."

"What firm?"

"Smith, Smith & Smith. I've no relation."

"Then you're not a Smith."

"No, I didn't mean that. I meant none of us Smiths are related to each other. Not brothers or anything like that."

"I see, what kinda law do you practice?"

"Tax and insurance."

"That's it?"

"Yep, that's it." [Bing, ru-rap] the elevator doors opened on the twelfth floor and no one is there either. The doors close and we're alone again.

"No murder cases?" I asked disappointed that only a tax, insurance lawyer was gonna help me with the Haynesville murders.

"No, just tax and insurance law, but I do sell used cars on the side."

"That's all I needed to hear. My heart sank to the floor. This guy has to be a nut case. No way was he gonna help me expose the murders.

"Why do you wanna help?" I asked.

"Let me explain, I met Rufus and his wife Amybelle at an insurance convention. We got to be great friends. Rufus made me executor of his estate in his Will. I tried to comfort Amybelle after he died, but it was no use. She went off the deep end and had to be placed in a mental institution. Rufus, being a successful insurance salesman, had set up a trust fund to take care of Amybelle and their son Rusty for the rest of their lives."

"That's good, but what's that got to do with the Haynesville murders?" I asked.

"Yeah, well this is the best part. What I found out going through his Insurance policy records while settling his estate is the best part." Another [Bing, ru-rap] from the elevator door opening interrupted our conversation.. A man got on and pushed the button for the lobby. Not another word was said. I stood there in silence anticipating what Wall Street Charlie would say about the best part. Soon we would be in the lobby alone where he could go on explaining about the best part. The ride down to the lobby seemed endless. It seemed like we would never get there. Another [bing, ru-rap] and the doors opened again. This time two more passengers got on for the ride to the lobby. Finally, the doors open into the lobby. Everyone got off except Wall Street Charlie and me.

"Push three," he said. I'm gonna get off there before we look too suspicious. You'd better go up to the tenth floor. We can't be seen together."

"No, you can't leave without telling me what you found in his Charity Life Insurance records. You just can't."

"Shoooh, calm down," whispered Wall Street Charlie. "We'll meet here again next monday. Elevator six. Say ten o'clock." [Bing, du-rap] the doors closed the curtain ending this play for the day. I rode back up to the tenth floor alone with my head spinning from the morning's events. Had Mr. Ball really shut down all investigations into the Haynesville murders? And Sheriff Tate's friend Officer Cuff. Is he in on the Haynesville murders too? This stranger on the elevator. Why is he trying to help me? With so many unanswered questions on my mind I didn't know what to do but stew in my frustration to expose the murders. Soon I was to have a most unexpected visitor and it was not going to be Wall Street Charlie.

Chapter 11

The Visitor

Having been led to believe Puddin was at a nurse's convention in Atlanta, I was alone at our Jonesboro home. Later I learned that was far from the truth. I was just beginning to sip an Old Fashion when the front door bell rang. Opening the door I was immediately confronted by two blue eyes outlined in thick mascara nestled in platinum blond hair staring at me.

"Hi there Dr. Rutherford," she sighed in a breathy voice from behind a high collared fox fur coat. "I'm Lovie. Remember me from Buck's apartment? You told me he was dead. Remember that?"

"Uh yeah," I said in disbelief that this high fashion woman, groomed to the hilt was Lovie. She looked nothing like the brassy girl I had seen in black laced underwear that night many years ago. Now she had to be in her fifties. A well preserved fifties.

"Well, that was me. Can we talk?" She asked pushing me aside with one thrust of her hip as she sashayed into the living room. "WOW!" she said excited by the sight of the Oriental carpet under her feet and the brightly polished brass chandelier hanging over her head. Then she turned to face the fire roaring in the fireplace, framed in thick oak paneling, and let out another, "WOW!

"Looks like Puddin's not here. May I take off my coat?"

"Heavens, how rude of me. Let me hang it up in the hall closet," I answered wondering how she knew Puddin was not home and how she found me after all these years. I had little time to ponder these questions when Lovie turned her back to me to slip off her fur coat. I grabbed it the instant it fell from her bare shoulders. It was so heavy it took both my hands to keep it from falling on the floor.

"Please sit down while I hang it up."

"Thank you. How nice to see you again and under such pleasant circumstances too," she said sliding into my favorite wingback tufted, leather chair by the fireplace.

"I'm drinking an Old Fashion. Would you like one?"

"Bourbon on the rocks will do fine."

I answered her request by taking a dusty bottle of Old Dog Bourbon off the shelf beside the fireplace. I had to chase it down for it had run at bay for years amongst the bottles of wine and sherry. I bought it long ago hoping Mr. Mathas would come up to Jonesboro someday and share it with me, but it never happened. Then I thought how strange it is for his mistress to be drinking it with me now.

"Here you go, Old Dog Bourbon on the rocks. It was Mr. Mathas' favorite as I'm sure you know."

The bourbon soaked ice cubes glittered like gold against the fire's orange-red flames.

"Thank you. Yum, yum this taste good. Just what I needed after traveling all day. Buck used to drink this bourbon all the time. And I do mean all the time," she said with a giggle.

I studied her as we sat there face to face in front of the fireplace. I dared not ask why she had come here for fear of offending her. Besides, I found her company quite pleasing. Our glances and glasses met and I sensed she wondered what to do next. I sat back and looked into the blue pools of her eyes. At that moment, our eyes had taken over where our words had failed and our silence had induced more intimacy than our words could ever express. From time to time, our arms moved in slow motion lifting the glasses to our lips. Sip-after-sip my eyes had drifted from her eyes and wondered down over her body and legs. Aroused by the experience, I continued my exploration and watched her lips pucker on the rim of her glass. The fire's glow was kind to her face. It concealed the wrinkles around her eyes and lips making her complexion appear smooth and vibrant. I sensed her anticipation wondering where my exploring eyes would go next. Hastening my exploration, she arched her back against the chair accenting her breast roaming free beneath her blouse. The thin silk blouse slipped back and forth across her erect nipples each time she lifted the glass to her lips. I followed the blouse down to where it disappeared underneath her tight white skirt's waistline. On cue, she slowly crossed her legs. My lusty gaze raced up her thighs. In one fleeting moment, I seen it all and my exploration had ended in a most arousing moment.

Separated by our anger toward each other, Puddin and I had lost our intimacy years ago. That had made me even more receptive to Lovie's seductive advances.

Yet, I resisted her advances and asked. "What do you want to talk about?"

Her answer had been physical not verbal. She kicked off her spiked heels and began rubbing her black stocking foot high up and down on my thigh.

"I just thought you'd like spending an evening with an old friend," she said slithering off the chair onto the floor. A motion that cause her skirt to slowly creep up around her waist causing her bareness to extend a most inviting invitation.

"I bet it gets lonely here without Puddin. Maybe it's even lonely when she's here. Huh? What you need is a real woman," she said while laying on the floor shamelessly swaying her naked thighs back and forth in the air. "Come on you handsome hunk, "Lovie pleaded. Give it to me. You know you wanna."

My question, what do you wanna talk about, had done nothing to break the mood. Seemed I was destined to plow ground Mr. Mathas had plowed before. I slid onto the floor and laid beside her with my sock feet pressing against her left cheek and her bare feet pressing against my right cheek.

"What kinda position is this?" Lovie asked. "I thought I had seen them all, but nothing like this one. Best let old Lovie take it from here," she said beginning to gyrate all over the floor. Her firm buttocks twitched in my hands as she tried to roll on top of me. "Ooooh, ooooh," she moaned. I tried to get to my feet. I knew if she got on top of me all was lost and I would be at her mercy.

"Don't you want me?" she asked in a breathy voice whispering over and over again in my ear. "Don't you want me?" Her legs spread apart and her pelvis slowly pulsating against my thigh had almost heightened my passion into submission. I could see why Mr. Mathas had enjoyed her company. She was his play pen and I just couldn't play in it. I had to break the mood and said in a calm voice, "let's stop it ain't gonna work. Don't be offended it's not you. It just ain't gonna work that's all."

Lovie's body went dead.

"What's wrong?" she asked getting up off the floor. I thought for a woman whose favors had never been rejected, she would be angry. Instead, she stood pathetically looking down at me laying at her feet. "Guess all this death around you has done a job on you huh? Since we're gonna do nothing, best get up off the floor and sit back down.

A leathery squeak came from the cushion in response to Lovie's bare bottom sliding across it. Lovie, half clad from the waist down, and me in my underwear settled down once again face to face in our wingback chairs in front of the fireplace.

"Get me another bourbon. I wanna tell you somethings about Haynesville's past that you need to know. Yep, I've been Buck's mistress ever since I was a legal eighteen. He's told me plenty about Haynesville over the years. Yep, plenty."

"Here you go," I said handing her a tall glass of Old Dog Bourbon and settling down in my chair with an Old Fashion. The mood was now different. No longer was my gaze lustful. And no longer was her gaze seductive. All this had passed. A new era had begun and I was curious to hear what she was itching to tell me..

"Please go on tell me what you know about Haynesville," I said. My request fell on deaf ears, for Lovie said nothing. I thought she had become too drunk to speak since I noticed her glass was empty. Suddenly, her voice broke the silence when she asked, "Hon make me another. Leave out the ice. Ain't nothing worse than pee water tasting bourbon."

I got her another bourbon and me another Old Fashion and sat back down waiting to hear what she had to say. .

Seemed like we would drink ourselves into oblivion before she would say anything. Her glass now half empty, she took a deep breath and began to speak.

. . . "You know there's never been any love between Buck and Vivian. I've heard tell Vivian was plumb eaten up with greed from the time she plopped from her mother's womb. She flirted around Buck till he got her pregnant and had to marry her. And that's how she got into the old Mathas family money. In fact, over the years, Buck hated her so much he became violent and took her out in the orchards to beat her and left her there all night. Some mornings the pickers would bring her home and some mornings they wouldn't.

"Gosh, that's awful. I've never heard that. Are you sure?"

"Sure I'm sure. Things finally got sorted out when Cleve became Vivian's lover and Buck settled in with me. Buck and Vivian lived peacefully after that. A good thing too because Puddin had seen more than her share of raw living. Thank goodness, Grandma Mathas had been there to comfort her through those dreadful years. "

"Lovie, I ain't never heard the likes of this. Are you sure it's not the bourbon talking instead of you?"

"I know it sounds mighty bad, but it's the truth."

"Has Mr. Mathas ever been mean to you?" I asked.

"Hell no. We understood each other. I liked his money and Buck well you know what he liked. Anyway, it's not Buck I wanna talk about. It's his half-brother."

"WHOOH!" Half brother?" I said shooting to my feet like a rocket blasting off to the moon. "I didn't know Mr. Mathas had a half-brother. Surely he would've mentioned it to me over the years."

"Yep, Buck's got a half brother."

"Who is he? Where does he live?""

"Pour me another bourbon and I'll tell you. Reckon my glass has a hole in it cause it's empty."

I got her another bourbon, but I wasn't about to drink another Old Fashion. My head had to be clear to hear this yarn about Mr. Mathas' half brother. Lovie took a few more gulps of bourbon and smacked her lips at its taste. She seemed most comfortable drinking and sitting half naked in her wingback leather chair. Obviously her life style had made her used to it.

"Well it's like this," she said. "They called Buck's daddy Big Buck and his son Little Buck to keep the two Bucks apart. You see Mr. Mathas' daddy was Big Buck and he was called Little Buck."

"Yeah, yeah I understand. Big Buck, Little Buck. Go on."

"Big Buck who was a young buck at the time liked the peach picking girls. I mean really liked them. Why he'd bang one every chance he got. Well doncha know? Nature took its course and a girl got pregnant and began to show. Now, there was nothing to do, but send her off to Jonesboro to hatch and that's what they did. And that's how Little Buck's half- brother came about. Light skin half brother I might add."

"So Mr. Mathas' half brother lives in Jonesboro."

"Yeah. Keep pouring the bourbon and I'll keep telling you more. Do you wanna hear more?"

"Heck yeah. What's his name?"

"Flavel Georgia named after our beloved peach state I suppose."

"FLAVEL! He can't be Big Buck's son. Why I've known him all my life. He drove the school bus when I was a kid. He lives right down the road from here. We see him all the time. He looks after our place when Puddin and I go to Haynesville. I can't believe we're talking about the same person."

She paused to finish her bourbon before saying anything else and sat waving her empty glass in the air. It was one o'clock in the morning and I dared not pour her another bourbon for fear she would pass out before telling me the rest of the story. However, after drinking a bottle of bourbon, her big blue eyes remained bright and her mind clear while my head was swimming in a sea of questions. Why had she come here? Why had she tried to seduce me? And why was she telling me about Flavel?

Lovie chuckled a few times and continued talking. "Well as it does, time passed and Flavel's mama moved back to Haynesville. There'd been no way for her son to come with her. She had to leave him behind to grow up in Jonesboro. Big Buck made sure his son Flavel had money to live on. Years later Flavel's mama married a man in Haynesville who stabbed Big Buck to death."

"What? I heard Mr. Mathas' daddy had a heart attack back in the 40s."

"No," Lovie explained. "Back then everybody knew Big Buck couldn't keep his hands off Flavel's mama. Big Buck's wife knew it too. The truth would've caused a horrible scandal later on so a heart attack satisfied everybody. So a heart attack it was."

"Damn what a story."

"Ain't no story. It's the Gospel truth. I'll swear it on a stack of Bibles."

"Even if it's true, why are you telling me now?"

"Ain't gonna say," she answered. "Let's just say I know what's going on in Haynesville and I feel mighty guilty about it too. Her eyelids began to droop and her Southern drawl got thicker. Old Dog Bourbon was beginning to take its toll. "I know if you don't stop messing around with that insurance company you're gonna get your balls busted real bad. That's why I had to come here and tell you about Flavel. He knows all about you going to the insurance company and he's telling the folks in Haynesville about it too. He had to or they would've killed his mama."

"You mean Flavel has known about me trying to expose the murders all these years? Is he in on it too?"

"I done told you Flavel's mama lived in Haynesville. You ought to have enough sense to know they've been talking to each other.

"Who's Flavel's mama? "I know most folks in Haynesville. Can't believe I never heard of Flavel's mama."

"You know, Soap Sally, "she answered.

"My God. You don't mean the woman who used to clean toilets at the Blue Bird Motel is Flavel's mama do you? I remember her when I sold peaches in Haynesville years ago. Called her Soap Sally because her hair looked like soap suds. Madam had her clean the Blue Bird Motel rooms every now and then. She was old then. Can't believe she's still alive. And I sure can't believe she's Flavel's mama."

"She was," said Lovie, "she had to be around eighty years old when she died. Flavel did everything he could to keep her alive. But that's not the real reason I'm here. Judge and the committee sent me here to seduce you and make you break Buck's Will so all your inheritance would go to them. Flavel told them you'd be alone tonight and they told me where you lived. I was to come here and make you be unfaithful to Puddin. Now I've told you everything I know. Once it became obvious I couldn't seduce you, I began to feel sorry for you. Buck loved you like a son. I know he wouldn't want anything to happen to you. I had to tell you everything so you won't get hurt."

"Lovie you gotta help me expose the murders before those cut throats kill us all."

"I wouldn't call them murders," she answered. An answer that had shocked me to the bone.

"Not murders. I call killing people for their insurance money murder. Wouldn't you?"

"No. I call it a sacrifice," Lovie answered, "some gotta die so folks in Haynesville can keep the only way of life they've ever known."

Those were her final words and her blue mascara lined eyes closed for the night. Old Dog Bourbon had taken its toll. I covered her with a quilt and went to bed. Lovie was gone when I awoke the next morning. Her visit had only made my nightmare worse. How could Flavel do this to me? Was he watching to see if I was seduced by Lovie? And why hasn't he come to help me expose the murders once his mama died? I had to find the answers to these questions. Hungover from my drunken night with Lovie I almost forgot **I had to meet Wall Street Charlie this morning.**

My head was still reeling in pain from the night's Old Fashions when I entered The Charity Life Insurance Building. I didn't look forward to riding my queasy stomach up-and-down the elevator either. [Bing] the elevator doors opened and I stepped into the number six elevator precisely at 10 o'clock as we had agreed and pushed the twelfth floor button. I stood there listening to the endless [Bings] on every floor. It seemed like everybody in the world got on and off the elevator that morning. A sweet old lady selling doughnuts in a zip-lock bag got on at the third floor. They smelled so good I had to buy one. Then two men got on at the fourth floor. I looked them over to make sure Wall Street Charlie hadn't taken on a disguise.

One was engrossed in reading the morning paper while the other whistled impatiently for the door to close. The elevator jerked up one more floor where the whistling man and the sweet old lady selling doughnuts got off. She thanked me profusely for buying a doughnut. Two women got on. It was like that all the way up to the twelfth floor. There the door opened and there stood Wall Street Charlie. He no longer looked like the scared little rabbit I had seen before.

"I'm gonna charge them all with **murder** and insurance fraud," he said in a stern voice as he charged into the elevator. His face was red and veins were popping out on his forehead. You could hear everyone on the elevator gasp in horror at the word murder. They scrambled to safety off the elevator at the next stop. Wall Street Charlie paid them no attention.

"Sheriff, Judge, Rev. and that funeral director Cleve. I especially hate that little worm. Anybody who's had a hand in these murders I want locked up for good."

Wall Street Charlie had named them all. Yet, I couldn't understand why he'd changed so much. He must know it's dangerous to challenge those cold blooded killers. I felt like hugging the guy. At last I found someone who would help me and he is full of piss and vinegar too.

"Why are you so fired up? I love it, but why?" I asked.

"Man this is my shot at the big time. Break this massive insurance fraud case and I'm sure to get a great job with Charity Life Insurance Co..

No more selling cars. I'll be a big shot Atlanta insurance salesman. This has gotta be the biggest crime ever committed in Georgia. And it's right here under my nose. I could be world famous. It's a dream come true. [Bing] the elevator doors open and the elevator fills up with people ending our conversation. The doors close and we descend in our silent little room non-stop to the lobby. I could tell he was extremely nervous and bit his tongue anxious to speak. The doors open and we stood there silent while the elevator deposited its human cargo into the lobby. Wall Street Charlie raced out of the elevator into the lobby and I followed after him.

"Wait. Where are you going? We gotta talk," I insisted.

"No time for that," he said rushing toward the front revolving doors, "got work to do. You get a witness and we'll talk. See you next Monday."

"Same place? Same time? I asked.

"Yes," he answered as he hurried out the door and disappeared into a crowd on the sidewalk.

Wall Street Charlie was right. I had to get a witness. At that moment I had no idea who it was to be. Thank goodness that moment was not to last long.

Chapter 12

The Witness

I've a witness and I shutter to think if it hadn't been for Lovie's visit I would have never found him. Now with his mother dead, there would be no reason why Flavel would not testify in court against those Haynesville cut throats. So, as soon as I left Wall Street Charlie that morning at the insurance company elevator I went to see him. Flavel had refused to live in his house once his wife died and moved into a trailer in his front yard beside 41 Hwy. It's a nice trailer painted like a giant Easter Egg with a wide red stripe going around its white exterior. He lives there alone with his only pet. A yellow school bus. It was now listing on its side because the tires were flat. The windows where I watched the seasons change were cracked and broken. Dandelions and rabbit tobacco weeds covered the doors where once laughing kids had scampered in and out of at each stop on their way to school.

However, the passing years had changed all my childhood memories. Now I must face my present reality and knock on his door. The curtains had been drawn tight over the small rectangular windows and it appeared no one was home. The cheap liquor bottles scattered around the trailer indicated he was grieving over his mother's death. A death without a funeral and a death he had never been allowed to mourn properly.

My knock caused a stirring movement inside the trailer. Its sound soon found its way to the front door. It opened and Flavel stood there his hair soaked and matted looking like he'd just been out in the rain. Water dripped from his tan colored hunting jacket and tattered bid jeans. His Brogan shoe soles were wet too. When he recognized me, a broad smile came over his sad face and he invited me inside his private world.

"Flavel you look mighty wet. Have you been out in the rain?"

"No," he smiled. "Been fixin' my toilet doncha know?"

"Got it fixed?"

"Don't look fixed does it?"

"No, guess not. We're gonna be gone in a few weeks. Sure would appreciate you looking after the place while we're gone. Oh, would you mind feeding Middleton while we're gone. We'll leave food out so it won't be much trouble."

"I'll do it."

I was extremely anxious, because the murders were more important than chitchatting about caretaking our home.

"Come let's sit at the table," Flavel said putting a cigarette between his teeth and lighting it with a match.

I began to panic anticipating my next question to Flavel. A question I had come to ask. So, after gathering up my courage, I leaned over the narrow kitchen table, looked him square in the eyes and asked,

"Flavel, what do you know about the Haynesville murders?"

Undisturbed by my question, he took a drag off his freshly lit cigarette, blew out the match and answered calmly, "Plenty."

His answer stunned me. Seemed he would have no problem talking about the murders. Then he paused a moment got up from the table and went over to the refrigerator where he took a swig from a bottle wrapped in a brown paper bag.

"I was wondering when you'd follow the trail to me, "he said as he came back to the table and crushed out his half smoked cigarette in the ash tray. Flavel's sad droopy eyes hung heavy on me as I asked,

"Do you know Lovie Summers?"

"Yeah."

Flavel hadn't volunteered any information, instead his answers were short and his stare cold.

"She paid me a visit the other night," I said. "We'd had a most interesting conversation."

"About what?" Flavel asked. Again his face was blank without expression and his stare cold.

"About you and your mama. You've been spying on me all the time I've been trying to expose the murders. Haven't you?" I gave Flavel no time to respond to my question and simply said, "I understand why you've become one of them. Lovie said they would kill your mama if you didn't do what they wanted you to do.

"She's right doncha know. I've been telling Judge Stoneridge and Sheriff Tate everything you've been doing all these years. You going to the insurance company and all. Sheriff Tate's a cold blooded killer. He held Mama hostage for years and threatened to kill her if I ever said anything about the murders. They should've at least let me be there when they buried her. It's time to get those cold blooded killers before they get me. How do we do it?" he asked getting up from the table to go back to the refrigerator and guzzle another swig of liquor from the bottle wrapped in a brown paper bag.

With the curtains drawn and clouds covering the mid morning sun, the kitchen was dark making the refrigerator light unusually bright. It shined on Flavel as if he was standing in the spotlight on a stage swigging the bottle. A disgusting cheap liquor smell began to fill the kitchen. Unable to tolerate this sight any longer, I said,

"Flavel come over here and sit down. We've got some serious thinking to do if we're gonna nail those bastards and it ain't gonna help if you keep getting liquored up. Tell me all you know about what's going on down there in Haynesville. I need to know because I'm gonna take that whole murdering gang to court and I need you to be a witness. Will you do that?"

"Yeah, yeah. But's there's a lot more you need to know before we do anything." It was obvious Flavel was getting more and more flustered about telling me all he knew. It was as if all the past years of his forced silence wanted to come busting out all at once.

"They killed Mr. Mathas," Flavel spurted out these words which came tumbling down on me like a crashing wave from the sea. Lost in its foam, I was so confused. I could hardly speak.

"That's not true. I was there. It was a mercy death. Mr. Mathas wanted to die. I heard Judge Stoneridge ask him if he wanted to die.

I saw Mrs. Pithum look at the paper pad beside Mr. Mathas. I saw his hand move the pen over the pad. And I saw her read what he'd written and tell the Judge 'Buck says yes'. I heard the heart monitor's beep stop while I was waiting for the nurse to unlock the door. I heard Mr. Mathas die."

"You heard what they wanted you to hear doncha know," said Flavel, "Mr. Mathas didn't wanna die. He wanted to live."

"How do you know that?"

"I was one of the hooded figures in the room. I could see through the eye-holes in my hood what he had really written. I'll never forget it."

I couldn't believe it. Flavel was one of the hooded figures and a member of the committee. He had been in the room the whole time Mr. Mathas died.

"Damn, Flavel. What did he write?"

"'HELP' that's what he wrote. 'HELP'. then he tried to write my name Flavel on the paper but he couldn't. He only got three letters on the paper. I know he was trying to spell my name. I know he was trying to ask me for help."

Unable to talk anymore about Mr. Mathas' death, Flavel broke down and began crying out loud. Tears rolled down his face as he sobbed openly. I consoled him and got him to pull himself together so I could go on talking about him being a witness.

"Flavel, get hold of yourself. There wasn't anything you or anyone else could've done for Mr. Mathas. He was old, his health gone and he would've never recovered from that stroke. He would've been unable to speak and paralyzed the rest of his life."

"Makes no difference," Flavel moaned as if in pain, "paralyzed or not Buck wanted to live."

"Calm down Flavel. Calm down," I repeated again and again. "We've got a lot to do and we can't do it if you're gonna get drunk and break down. Do you hear me? Do you hear what I'm saying?"

"I hear you."

"Well then. Go on tell me what you know."

Flavel finally gets a grip on his emotions and begins to talk. "It's like this. The committee that's mainly Judge Stoneridge, Cleve, Vivian, Rev. Boswell."

"Come on Flavel," I interrupted, "I know who the committee is. Will you testify against them? That's what I wanna know."

"I will, but you have to listen to what I'm saying. The committee knows you're trying to expose them to the Charity Insurance Co. cause I told them you was. Doncha know?"

"Yeah, I know all that. Go on."

"Well, that's made them powerful nervous and that's when Vivian decided to use Mr. Mathas's death to her advantage and get you under her thumb. She wanted you on her side. She wanted you to join in on planning the murders. She sensed your greed to inherit the land. That's why she made sure you inherited the land. She thought you'd kill to keep it too."

"She was almost right," I answered.

"Yeah," said Flavel, "I thought you might join them too. What changed your mind?"

"All those people being so brutally murdered. I just can't stand it. Won't anyone do anything about it either. The land is useless without a peach crop. I tried to tell them that, but they wouldn't listen. I wanted to make the land pay off and build Peach Land, but they wouldn't let me. If they had, I don't know what I would have done. I hate to think about it.

Flavel shook his head and said, "that amusement park idea made them mad. Even madder than you going to the insurance company. Sheriff Tate's been waiting his chance to kill you and he almost got it when you started talking about bull dozing down those peach trees. They're like their own children to folks in Haynesville. Shucks, to some I say more important for they would kill their own kin for money to save the orchards and their way of life. Yep, holy ground to folks in those parts."

"Flavel, that's what you've gotta say in court. You gotta testify how they've made murders look like accidents. You gotta testify how the committee created this scheme to get money to keep Haynesville alive all these years."

"I'll tell them," said Flavel, "But will anyone believe me?"

"I don't know, but we've gotta keep trying or more innocent people will die including us."

"Don't make no difference in my case," said Flavel, "look around. I ain't got much to live for anyway."

"Great. That's all I need is for you to get pitiful on me. We're gonna clean that mess up down there in Haynesville and you're gonna get some backbone and help me. We'll start by taking the sting out of the scorpion. And that's the committee. I'm gonna have my friend come by and see you. I want him to know I've got a witness. He's a lawyer and all fired up about solving these crimes. If all three of us band together, we can do it. We can clean that mess up." Flavel just grunted at my words and remained seated at the kitchen table. I was not surprised by his next words,

"Uh, your wife's in on it too. Doncha know?"

"I suspected that all along," I answered. "Is she in on planning any new murders?"

"Don't know. I've just been sitting around here since Mama died waiting for Sheriff Tate to come and kill me."

"Listen to me Flavel. Don't worry about Sheriff Tate. Long as you're up here in Jonesboro you're safe. I doubt he'll kill anyone outside of Orchard County. You'll talk to my friend won't you?"

"Yes. What's his name?"

"Don't know yet," I was embarrassed to say., "I call him Wall Street Charlie. He hasn't given me his name. He's like you afraid someone will kill him and wants to keep his identity secret. Don't worry. We'll all plan our case together. I'll see him in the morning.

Chapter 13

The Junk Yard Meeting

The next morning I was riding the elevator at the insurance company and couldn't wait to see Wall Street Charlie because I now had Flavel as my witness. At any second I had expected to see him pop into the elevator as the doors opened. But, he hadn't. This was my third meeting with him and I had ridden the elevator so much that the sweet old lady selling doughnuts, the five young women darting in and out like schools of fish and the man reading the morning paper were now smiling at me and saying good morning like I was an old friend. [Bing] The elevator doors opened on the twelfth floor and there was Wall Street Charlie. He got into the elevator with four other people and the doors closed. I moved over to him and stuck a piece of paper in his pocket. It contained Flavel's name, address, telephone number and witness information.

Then I said, "we can talk now. I have a witness. All his information is on that paper I just gave you."

My speaking to him in front of all these people must've startled him because he jumped off the elevator at the next stop when the doors opened and ran out of the building. I left the elevator thinking I had scared Wall Street Charlie off for good. Thank goodness I was wrong because the telephone rang that evening.

"Hello," I answered.

"Dr Rutherford," a reluctant voice replied. It sounded familiar, but it was fuzzy and I had not recognized it at first.

"Yes, I'm Dr. Rutherford."

"We need to meet now in my office."

"Who is this?" I asked.

"Oh, I'm sorry," a voice answered, "It's me the lawyer in the elevator. My name is Charlie. Charlie Smith."

My mind got side tracked for a fleeting moment. I couldn't believe it. "Wall Street Charlie's name is really Charlie," I mumbled. I guess he heard my mumbling over the phone for he asked.

"What did you say?"

"Never mind. So, your name is really Charlie?"

"Yeah, yeah, its Charlie. We gotta meet now. I heard you say you had a witness. You've gotta come to my office so we can plan his deposition. Our lives depend on it."

Charlie gave me the directions to his office over the phone and I wasted no time getting there. He was right. Smith, Smith& Smith was a small law firm. I followed the signs and drove my car through rows of junked cars to the office. Some cars were without wheels, some without windshields and some so battered you couldn't even tell if they had ever been cars. I began to see why he was so eager to solve the murders. Getting a job at the Charity Insurance Co. would be a gigantic leap forward out of this junk yard. I was beginning to wonder if I would ever find Charlie's office amongst all of this junk when I spotted him running down the road towards me waving his arms in all directions. Finally his arm motions began to make sense as he directed me into something that looked like a giant refrigerator. It had a sign on it "BAKED PAINTING". His lips were moving, but I couldn't hear a word he was saying until he got closer. He was telling me to pull my car into the giant refrigerator. I followed his direction and said, "I thought we were done with all this high level secrecy."

"We are. I just wanna take a few last minute precautions. Please indulge me." "Will anybody paint my car if I park it here? I want it a canary yellow if they do."

"Don't be silly," said Charlie, " nobody is gonna bother your car. Hey, look at the good side. We're off the elevator and I've all the doughnuts you can eat at the office."

I did my best to keep up with Charlie and followed him passed cars in various stages of repair.

"Follow me," he said, "we're going over to the other lot. My office is over there." It took all my breath and strength to hustle along side Charlie as we walked from this dingy dark junk yard toward a used car lot lit up like broad day light by hundreds of clear glass light bulbs strung over head.

Flapping in the breeze were red, white and blue triangular shaped flags intermingled between the light bulbs. Every now and then a gust of wind would send the flags flapping so loud it sounded like a covey of quail taking flight. No matter how old they were, all the lights made the used cars look shiny and new. I kept following Charlie until we finally stopped in front of a doll house complete with a bent stove-pipe chimney sticking out of its ginger bread roof, petite flower boxes in its tiny windows and a child sized door. . . . Chasing after Charlie left me gasping for air as I stood there looking up at the sign extending upward off the doll house roof. It was so huge it looked as if the house was attached to it rather than the sign attached to the house. It read: UNCLE TOM'S USED CARS.

"Come on in," said Charlie.

At his invitation, I stooped over and crouched my way through the door into a room small as the elevator. He followed me and we both sat there on the floor facing each other with our arms draped over our knees.

"Is this your real office?"

"Yeah. Isn't it unique? I know it's crazy to most folks, but I just couldn't sell it when my daughter died. So, I kept it and use it as an office."

"It's different," I said looking around at the furnishings. Four metal filing cabinets pushed up against the walls were the only furniture in the doll house. None were marked insurance files and none were marked tax files. All were marked repossessions. The junk yard, body shop, used car lot and now a doll house office full of car repossession files made me think Charlie was crazy. No way was this weird guy going to help me expose the murders. If anything, he's gonna make it worse. In my darkest despair, I asked.

"Charlie, are you sure you're an insurance lawyer?"

"Well, not exactly," he answered. "I admit I've stretched the truth a bit. If I hadn't you never would have believed I could help you. But I am a lawyer," he said pointing to a framed diploma hanging on the wall. "And I've passed the Georgia Bar too," he added pointing to another diploma hanging on the wall. Both looked enormous in relationship to the small doll house wall. "I can practice any kind of law

I want. Murder, insurance fraud it doesn't matter. And that's what I'm gonna do."

"Okay," I agreed. I wasn't gonna argue with him. After all he was the only one willing to help me. It was time to settle down and plan our case against the committee. "I've a witness. A damn good one too," I said.

"Great," said Charlie, getting all excited and bouncing around inside the doll house so much I thought it would fall off its foundation. That's what we need. Who is it?"

"His name it Flavel Georgia. We gotta go see him in the morning."

A tapping sound on the front door interrupted our conversation. This was followed by a raspy voice saying.

"Charlie, I've gotta get in there. Got a customer out here who needs to sign some papers. Are yawl about done?"

"IN A MINUTE !" Charlie shouted.

"Who's that?" I asked.

"That's Tom . . . Tom Smith. "Sounds like he needs the office. We'd best go."

"Wow! Yawl really do use this doll house as an office." I grunted squeezing my stooped over body out the child sized door. "What do you do with a really fat customer?" I asked jokingly only to see this really hefty lady coming our way. Charlie wasn't about to answer that question. He saw the fat lady the same time I did and was about to bust out laughing. We both scooted out the door into the used car lot and busted out laughing. I was laughing so hard I failed to notice how Tom and the fat lady had gotten through the door into the doll house. And I pictured in my mind them sitting on the floor together and couldn't stop laughing. Charlie's law office was certainly unlike anything I've seen before.

Early next morning I picked Charlie up at the used car lot and went to see Flavel. I knocked on the trailer door and while awaiting his arrival at the door I noticed all the liquor bottles were cleaned up from around the trailer. I noticed something else too. The school bus was no longer listing on its side and the tires were no longer flat.. He had also cleared the tall grass, dandelions and rabbit-tobacco weeds away from the bus and it was now sporting a fresh coat of yellow paint. A can of black paint was sitting on the ground next to the bus awaiting Flavel's skillful hands to trim it in the words Cedar County Schools. It seemed like no one would come to the door and Charlie's hands began fidgeting in and out of his pockets. Then he began thumping one foot and then the other on the steps. I just stood there looking at the school bus remembering the magical times I had on it when suddenly the door opened abruptly and Flavel greeted us with a cheery, "Good morning. I've been expecting yawl. Please come in."

"Good morning Flavel. I want you to meet Charlie Smith of Smith, Smith & Smith law firm. No relation," I said winking at Charlie. "Charlie this is Flavel Georgia." As they shook hands, I couldn't help but notice how Flavel's clothes had changed. Gone was the hunting jacket and tattered bib-jeans. In their place was a freshly starched and ironed long sleeve blue Oxford cloth shirt with its coller buttoned down neatly around his neck. Its blue color showed off Flavel's crystal clear blue eyes which were a far cry from the red swollen eyes that had greeted me the other day. His khaki pants looked as if they had just been washed and ironed. His hair was no longer wet and matted. It was dry and neatly combed. Charlie and I entered the trailer and were instantly greeted by the aroma of brewing coffee and the sound of bacon sizzling in the frying pan.

"Yawl got here just in time for breakfast."

"Good," said Charlie, "I'm hungry."

"Me too. Flavel you'll never know how relieved I am that you took my advice," I said. There'd been no need to mention what advice. He knew I meant his drinking. "And the school bus. I see you're restoring it. It looks fantastic just like it used to look when I rode it."

"Oh yeah, that old bus is a lot like me. We both needed restoring. It weren't rusted bad as I thought. Then again neither was I."

"What's all this talk about a school bus? Charlie asked.

He was already sitting at the small gray formica topped table buttering up a piece of toast and smothering it with a sizeable helping of strawberry jam.

"Flavel drove the school bus when I was growing up here in Jonesboro."

"He did?"

"Yep," I answered pulling out one of the chrome piped chairs padded in gray flowered vinyl from under the table and sat down.

Flavel hosted us with coffee, orange juice, grits, bacon and sunny side up eggs. "Must've opened and closed them school bus doors thousands of times a day," said Flavel while pouring Charlie more coffee. "Each time them doors opened I tell them kids to hurry up and get on the bus. Can't wait all day gotta get home to feed the cows and pay my bills. I know'd they'd paid me no mind. They'd scamper up the steps and go squirming down the aisle to their seats. Their chattering voices got louder and louder at each stop as more and more kids got on the bus. I thought I would go on hauling them kids back and forth to school forever, but things have a way of changing."

"That's for sure," Charlie shook his head in agreement as he swallowed a big mouth full of grits. I thought to myself, for a skinny man he could sure put the vittles away.

"Why," said Flavel, "I never believed that little boy named Poon I picked up each morning would someday go off to medical school and become Dr. Rutherford."

"And I never thought my school bus driver would be helping me solve the Haynesville murders either," I said. "Charlie, I think Flavel is gonna make a fine witness."

"Enough about all that," exclaimed Charlie, "yawl can't keep carrying on and getting nostalgic and crying in your coffee over some old school bus. We've got work to do."

Flavel never got to eat breakfast that morning. Every time he brought the fork to his mouth, Charlie asked him another question. Flavel finally gave up and just sat there staring at this skinny little man with the bull's eye target eyes. And as usual, Charlie was sharply dressed in a blue pin-striped suite and a narrow red and blue striped tie. His salt and pepper gray hair was neatly parted to one side and combed down over his forehead and trimmed around his ears. Charlie spent all morning taking Flavel's deposition while I sat there drinking orange juice. It was a laborious process since Charlie had to write down every word Flavel said by hand. The deposition was boring until I heard Flavel say.

"Put Sheriff Tate on the stand and he'll have to name everyone on the committee including me and Dr. Rutherford's wife. That would mean we'd both go to jail."

Flavel was right. He had been talking to Sheriff Tate all those years he was spying on me. A fact which had made him part of the committee. My breakfast no longer interested me. I had to listen to what else Flavel was gonna tell Charlie and it was an ear full.

“It all started years ago,” said Flavel, “with Cleve the funeral director. He’s been Vivian’s. Uh, Vivian that’s Mr. Mathas’ wife.”

“Yes, yes. I know her. I know who she is.” said Charlie.

“Well, like I was saying. Cleve’s been her lover long as I can remember. Mr. Mathas knew it too. He’d beat her something awful when he’d hear tell they’d been together. But that didn’t stop Vivian. She’d do anything for Cleve and has done it too. It was Cleve’s idea to kill people for their insurance money to run Haynesville once the money dried up. But he couldn’t organize it like Vivian could. She got Judge Stoneridge, Rev. Boswell and all Haynesville’s prominent citizens to go along with Cleve’s idea. She planned the murders and got Sheriff Tate to carry them out. Yep, Vivian was the brains behind the whole thing and she loved it because Cleve loved her for doing it. That woman would’ve done anything for that man doncha know.”

“Yeah, yeah,” once again Charlie interrupted. “I know all about that. But keep going. I’m listening.”

I was amazed how much Charlie knew about the Haynesville murders. I couldn’t help but wonder how he found out about them and why he had done nothing to stop them.

“They won’t ruin any more lives when we’re done with them,” said Charlie. “Now tell me about Dr. Rutherford’s wife. Why do you think she’s tolerated all this for so long and where does she fit into this mess? I’ve gotta know all the facts.”

“I don’t rightly know,” Flavel answered. “Guess she’s seen how awful her daddy treated her mother and how happy she was with Cleve. Guess she just wanted her mother to be happy. That’s all.

She ain't got the guts her mother had. She'll never be able to save Haynesville."

"What do you mean?" Charlie asked.

Flavel looked across the table at me as if to ask my permission to speak further about my wife. I nodded go ahead.

"All right then. She's involved in the committee meetings since her mother died. That's all I know."

Charlie stopped scratching down Flavel's words on the yellow legal pad with his ball-point pen and laid it down on the table in front of him and said sternly, "Flavel this ain't no game we're playing here. This is a murder trial we're getting ready for. I don't have to tell you we're up against lunatics who'd just soon kill you as look at you. So don't hold back anything. I've gotta know all the facts if we're gonna win this case. Now, do we understand each other or not?"

Shocked by Charlie's sudden out burst Flavel and I answered in unison, "We do."

"Okay then," said Charlie, "go on tell me about Dr. Rutherford's wife. How is she involved in the committee meetings? Has she planned any murders?"

"No," Flavel answered, "we gotta stop her before she's in it too deep doncha know?"

"We gotta stop a lot of things," said Charlie, "that's why I've already scheduled a preliminary hearing at the Orchard County Courthouse."

"You've done **WHAT!?**" I lashed out at Charlie for this was a surprise.

"Oh yeah. I had decided to go it alone," Charlie answered. "But now with you and Flavel I can make a better case against them. We need all the evidence we can get. We gotta be ready by next week. I'll get a car off the used car lot and we'll go down there together."

"You mean Haynesville?" I asked still dazed by Charlie's sudden decision to confront the committee. "That's Orchard County. Judge Stoneridge's court. We can't go there. That'd be like going into the devil's mouth. The Judge will chew us up and spit us out for sure."

"Got to," Charlie snapped back, "we gotta go and formally charge them with murder and fraud. That's the law. If we all stick together, we can't lose. Are you with me?"

Charlie's question made me feel sick and scared. I think Flavel did too. Charlie was right, but his lightning pace for getting things done unnerved me.

"Do yawl agree?" Charlie asked again. His words rang in my ears like all the bells on New Year's Eve. He was right. No matter if it cost me my wife, my inheritance and my life. I knew it had to be done. I answered,

"Yeah, I agree."

"Fine with me," said Flavel.

Charlie got up from the table, folded the yellow pages flat on the legal pad and tucked it under his left arm. With his right hand, he picked up a piece of toast off the table and took a bite out of it and said, "We'll meet back here tomorrow if that's all right with yawl? We'll do all our preparations right here. I like it. It's quiet and out of the way. No one will know what we're doing."

"What about Puddin?" I asked, "I gotta tell her what we're doing. I'm sure she's suspicious."

"Not a word," Charlie said placing his index finger over his lips."

"But Puddin is my wife," I tried to explain to Charlie.

"Don't matter," Charlie said in a rude voice, "Until we get this case won we're not talking to anyone outside this circle and that includes your wife. From what Flavel told me she's not to be trusted."

"I hate to say it, but you're right. I'll say nothing." I knew Puddin had been traveling back and forth from Jonesboro to Haynesville by herself after her mother's death. She told me she was settling her mother's estate, but I had suspected she was getting involved with the committee. My thoughts about Puddin were interrupted when I felt something kicking my leg from under the table. It was Flavel. Guess he sensed I was getting down in the dumps.

"Cheer up," he said. "Things have gotta change and we've gotta change with them. Look at me. I'm gonna have this trailer hauled off and I'm gonna move back in the house. What do you think about that?"

"That's great," I said," stand up and give me a hug. When this is all over, I want a ride in the school bus too."

"You'll get it," Flavel said as we stood there with our arms wrapped around each other. "I'll pick you up like I used to. I still remember the route doncha know. We'll ride it together."

"Oh Lord," groaned Charlie," there yawl go again. I best be going. Got work to do back at the car lot. Uh, I mean the law firm."

Charlie and I left Flavel's trailer that morning feeling confident the hearing would go well. I was confident Charlie would be the white knight who would lead us to victory. But I was in for a big surprise.

Chapter 14

The Hearing

Two more miles and we'll be on Hwy 42 going toward the Peach Blossom Trail. Flavel, Charlie and I had just been down that road a week ago to attend the hearing. Now I'm driving down it with Puddin. I saw Charlie in action at the hearing and knew it was just a matter of time before he would put her behind bars with the others.

The hearing went better than I had ever dreamed it would. Clad in a black robe, Judge Stoneridge was already on the bench when Charlie, Flavel and I arrived at the Orchard County Courthouse that afternoon. The courtroom was full of people. Each one turned in their seat to glare at us as we entered through the courtroom door. I dared not look them in the eye for I had no idea who they were. I didn't think we would have a place to sit until I heard Judge Stoneridge say, "Yawl come up front. There's a table waiting for you up here beside Sheriff Tate." Following the Judge's directions, we went and took our seats next to Sheriff Tate and a nondescript looking man, who I assumed was his lawyer. We all sat at a small oak table in front of the Judge's bench. Mrs. Bebe Pithum, Orchard County's

Court recorder, sat next to us. I had never seen the courtroom in daylight since my previous encounter with it had been in total darkness the night I robbed Judge Stoneridge's files for the termination list. The courtroom and jury box appeared smaller than I expected. Its wooden rail was shorter than the endless one I ran my fingers along in the dark that night.

"Good morning your honor," said Charlie..

"Mornin'," the Judge responded.

All eyes immediately fell on Charlie cooking the moment to a high temperature. Charlie, boiling in all his glory, stood holding a shiny black leather briefcase in his hands. He was dressed impeccably in a gray and blue pin-striped suit divided in the middle by a solid yellow neck tie. The highly polished leather Italian loafers he was wearing matched his briefcase perfectly. It was a sight to see. Wall street Charlie was on stage at The Orchard County Courthouse. His round rimmed glasses and distinguished salt and pepper hair had given him a big city lawyer mystic image. It did not matter to him that his law firm had its office in a doll house in a used car lot and his real specialty was selling and repossessing used cars. What mattered now was what the Judge was gonna say about this intruder standing before him. To my surprise, the Judge squinted down at him and simply said, "state your case."

"Yes your honor," said Charlie, "let the record show my name is Charlie Smith and I am here as Dr. Rutherford's attorney. As you know, we've petitioned this court for this preliminary hearing to officially charge Sheriff Tate and other members of this community with insurance fraud and conspiring to commit murder. Multiple murders. And I've reason to believe, even though Sheriff Tate was doing what he was told to do, it was his hands that did the killing."

Then Charlie looked over at Mrs. Pithum to make sure she was typing every word he was saying. His words had caused a murmur of muffled tones from the crowd which soon escalated into a loud booing, hissing chorus. It got so loud that the Judge started banging his gavel on the bench to shut them up.

"Here, here," the Judge said banging down the gavel louder and louder on the bench, "Dr. Rutherford has brought these people all the way down here from Jonesboro. Least we can do is show them some of Haynesville's hospitality. This caused the crowd to hush up and a deafening silence fell upon the room like a wet blanket snuffing out a fire.

"That's better. Now go on Mr. Smith."

"Yes your honor. Today I want to focus on Sheriff Tate. I'll get to the other committee members later. And I want to charge him with cold blooded murder." This caused another outburst from the crowd. Again the room erupted in a sea of booing and hissing sounds. I turned around to see members of the crowd shaking their angry fists in the air. And again the Judge started banging his gavel down on the bench to quiet them down.

"And Sheriff Tate how do you plead?" asked the Judge looking over at Sheriff Tate.

There was no immediate answer and Sheriff Tate remained silent. Instead, a man wearing a white shirt, white pants and a solid white neck tie rose from his chair beside Sheriff Tate. His dark eyebrows quivered up and down a few times before being drawn into a frown. His fingers raked through his oily black hair and writhed about his neck like a snake. They finally slithered down his chest and crawled across the table in front of him knocking a few papers off the table to the floor. Quickly, his nondescript face, composed of generic eyes, nose and mouth, disappeared beneath the table as he bobbed up and down picking up the papers. He came up from under the table after gathering the papers off the floor, gasped for air and said, "not guilty, your honor."

"Counsel," said the Judge pointing his knobby arthritic finger at Charlie. "You may present the court with the evidence against the defendant Sheriff Tate."

"Alright your honor. May I present exhibit A?"

"You may."

"This exhibit called the termination list is to be introduced as exhibit A. I call it the termination list because it has the title termination written right up here at the top," Charlie said while waving the paper in the air for all to see. "I'll show the court that the names on the tomb-stones in the peach orchards match those on this list. Here your honor let me give you this list. Note I have all the death certificates attached to it too," Charlie said as he darted up to Judge Stoneridge and neatly placed the papers before him on the bench. "Furthermore, I'll show the court how the names got on this list and how those people got under those tombstones out there in the orchards and who put them there. In fact, he's right here in this courtroom and he's sitting right there," Charlie said pointing his finger in Sheriff Tate's face. Again the crowd booed and hissed and this time the Judge made no attempt to stop their loud angry shouts. His head sank low on his chest. His eyes darted back and forth between Charlie and Sheriff Tate. And, with his arms folded in front of him, the Judge began to take on the look of a guilty child about to be spanked by the swift hand of the law.

In a flash, Sheriff Tate's lawyer sprang up from his seat and shouted, **"I OBJECT**!!"

"YEAH! YEAH!" The crowd began to chant. "WE OBJECT!"

Bang! Bang! the Judge banged his gavel down on the bench trying to quiet the crowd. The crowd's voices melted into silence as they awaited his verdict. "**Sustained**," the Judge said which caused the crowd to go shouting again. "YEAH! YEAH!"

Sheriff Tate's lawyer waved his arms around in the air to hush the crowd and said, "This termination list Judge. Wasn't it stolen from your office. Wasn't it in your private files?"

"Yes," the Judge answered withhis head held high like he had just won an olympic gold medal.

"I say it cannot be admitted as evidence against my client until we find out who robbed your office."

"I agree. That's a serious matter," said the Judge, "remove exhibit A the termination list from the record."

Charlie remained calm and humbly asked the Judge, "May I present exhibit B, your honor?"

"You may."

"Exhibit B is a sworn affidavit by Mr. Flavel Georgia stating he has witnessed Sheriff Tate and the committee planning the murders of those on the termination list. It also states how Sheriff Tate and the committee have held Flavel hostage for years by threatening to kill his mama if he ever said anything about the Haynesville murders."

"**I OBJECT!**" Sheriff Tate's lawyer shouted. Strangely enough, there was no out cry from the crowd supporting his objection. They remained silent awaiting the Judge's response.

"Sustained," he said.

"Thank you your honor," said Sheriff Tate's lawyer bowing politely toward the Judge. "Who is this Flavel Georgia? And why should we believe anything he says?" he asked turning toward the crowd in the courtroom.

To which the crowd responded, "YEAH! YEAH!"

"Has anyone here ever seen this Flavel Georgia in Haynesville?" asked Sheriff Tate's lawyer as he waved his hands around Flavel's face as if to frame it in a picture.

"NO! NO!" the crowd shouted back in response to his question. "Well then I see no reason why this court should believe anything from this stranger. Your honor may I ask Mr. Flavel Georgia where he resides?"

"You may."

"Mr. Flavel Georgia tell this court where you live."

"Jonesboro," Flavel answered meekly.

"Yes, and how long have you lived there?"

"All my life," answered Flavel so quietly you could hardly hear him. This prompted Sheriff Tate's lawyer to say, "speak up man I can hardly hear you. I say again how long have you lived in Jonesboro?"

"All my life," Flavel answered in a louder voice.

"Your honor I want this exhibit B removed from the record. This man obviously has no connection with Haynesville and there's no way he could see Sheriff Tate do anything wrong."

"So granted," said the Judge. Mrs. Pithum please remove both exhibits A and B from this hearing's records."

Mrs. Pithum's eyes peered up at the Judge through the netted veil on her pill box hat and she said, "yes your honor."

One last time, the crowd chanted, "YEAH! YEAH!"

Bang, bang. Judge Stoneridge banged his gavel down on the bench and announced," this hearing is closed."

Chapter 15

The Last Meeting

It's 6 o'clock and the sun is slowly sinking behind Puddin's mountainous form. My only source of conversation continues to be the car engine's drone. Will Puddin ever speak to me again? If so, what will she say? Forty five miles ahead lies the exit to Hwy. 42 going to the Peach Blossom Trail. Little time is left for us to reconcile our feelings toward each other. Little time is left for us to work together and heal Haynesville's wounds inflicted by its evil desperation. Instead, time, our ideals, and fate have put us on a collision course. Her's is to fulfill the promise made to her mother that she'll never let Haynesville become another Pennyfield no matter what the cost. Mine is to destroy that promise and expose the murders. But I have failed to destroy her promise and now I am at the mercy of the Haynesville community. I knew it was just a matter of time before Sheriff Tate comes knocking like he has done before. I knew he would never rest until I am either dead or a member of that deadly committee. **That sound still haunts me. It was just a simple** Knock! Knock! Knock!

It happened that evening after the hearing. Charlie and Flavel had gone back to Jonesboro. I stayed in Haynesville waiting for Puddin to come down so we could finish settling her mother's affairs. I was alone in the house when Sheriff Tate drove his car into the driveway. The sight of that cold blooded killer in the courtroom had made my skin crawl and now he was knocking on the back porch screen door. Paranoid thoughts raced through my mind. He has come to kill me. Why had I stayed here alone? Why hadn't I gone back to Jonesboro with Charlie and Flavel?

KNOCK! KNOCK! KNOCK!

His knocking was so loud I could tell it was from strong hands. Hands capable of snapping my spine in a twitch of his wrist. I had to get those thoughts out of my mind, for surely Sheriff Tate had not come to kill me.

KNOCK! KNOCK! KNOCK!

Finally, I mustered enough courage to enter the dark back porch where I saw Sheriff Tate's body silhouetted against the moon lit sky. His broad-brimmed hat, knee high boots, and the silver whistle hanging from his shirt pocket made him appear more like a law officer than a cold blooded killer.

KNOCK! KNOCK! KNOCK!

He had failed to see me in the dark even though I was only a short distance away from him. The knocking stopped and I was about to come face to face with Haynesville's cold blooded killer. Fear welled up in my stomach like a rotten oyster as the screen door opened inch by inch. The man who arranged Merietta's decapitation and The Flint River Bridge Wreck was about to poke his head into the back porch. He would soon pull the bead chain, hanging from the ceiling, to turn on the light and expose my presence.

My chest throbbed and my heart pumped blood throughout my trembling body. Certainly Sheriff Tate hadn't planned to kill me here on the back porch.

The light flashed on with an ear piercing CLICK bathing his face in a yellow bug light glow. Calmly, I wiped the long sleeve of my shirt across my forehead to wipe off the sweat, because I did not want to appear scared.

"What-cha-say? Let's go," he said in a toothy grin.

"Go where?"

"To the hospital. I told Judge Stoneridge you were still in town. He wants to see you. He sent me to get you. So let's go."

Like two monks in a vow of silence we entered the hospital and took the elevator up to the unmarked floor. The same floor on which they had killed Mr. Mathas a year ago. We entered the door marked Toxic Waste where Judge Stoneridge stood awaiting our arrival. He greeted me with a slap on the back and lip smacking laugh.

"Come on in here you red headed devil you. Ha-ha," he laughed wiping his mouth with a napkin.

His nose was redder than usual and a bourbon odor accompanied his joviality. "You little runt devil. Looks like you wanna give us some rough water down here in Haynesville. We've been waiting for you."

The Judge was drunk and from the drippy-yellow stains on his white linen shirt his drinking had gotten sloppy. His tom-foolery had both scared and amazed me. I was shocked by the appearance of the room in which Mr. Mathas had died. Nothing had changed. The medical paraphernalia and bed he died in were still there. And the same group was gathered around the bed again --- Judge Stoneridge, Rev. Boswell, Mr. Speckman, Cleve Elderidge and the Pithums. Only this time they were gayly laughing and sprawled out in folding aluminum lounge chairs like they were sunning on a beach. Only one hooded figure was in the room. Flavel had been right he was one of the hooded figures which made me wonder who is this one.

"Come," urged the Judge. "Sit your skinny butt by me."

His words triggered more laughter. Unlike the others, the Judge took a seat in a lazy boy recliner. "Come on you little runt devil sit by me. I ain't gonna bite. I might pinch but I ain't gonna bite. "Ho, ho, ha, ha," he started laughing again. "You remember Bebe. our court recorder. Oh Hell, you know everybody here."

Mrs. Bebe Pithum still wore a blue and white poky dotted dress. However, this time it was rumpled like she had been sleeping in it and its hem was above her knees exposing her garter rolled top stockings.

The pillbox hat, that once sat squarely atop her head, was cocked over her right ear with its veil askew. No longer were her fingers poised on the typewriter keys waiting to record every word. Now the typewriter was a forgotten relic sitting on the floor next to her feet. It was obvious. She was drunk too.

"How are you doing?" I asked politely.

She shyly giggled and smiled as she looked up at me and answered, "fair to middlin'."

Again the Judge's knobby arthritic fingers began rippling through the air as if playing an imaginary piano. His fingers stopped on the last note and pointed to Mr. Pithum as he said, "Go Roy, Go." At the sound of the Judge's words, Mr. Pithum got up and started doing the peppermint twist. I thought it strange since there was no music playing. His dark blue suit coat was off, his shirt collar unbuttoned and his pin striped red and yellow neck tie hung loosely around his neck.

"How are you doing?" I asked never expecting him to answer.

"Ain't doing worth a damn. Can't get it up any more. Bebe'll tell you. Tell him Bebe. Don't make no difference. How I do envy them youngons down yonder poking them cows. Must take a heep to poke a cow. Why I ---"

"Uh, Roy," the Judge butted in, "we'll hear about them cows some other time," the Judge said. "Hold that thought. We'll get to it later. Right now we gotta do what we came here to do."

"Yeah, what's that?" Asked Mr. Speckman. "Pass that bottle over here Bebe will you honey. Hearing about yawls sex life calls for another drink." A titter of laughter went through the group and their heads bobbed up and down in agreement.

"Shut up, I'm trying to conduct a serious meeting here," the Judge commanded.

"Okay then let's get to it," Mr. Speckman agreed. "We all got one experience in common and that's death. If we don't get going we're all gonna share it with this here Rutherford rat." His whimsy caused another titter among the group.

The Judge leaned over and looked me straight in the eye and asked, "Dr. Rutherford do you recall the Will reading here when Buck died?"

"I do indeed."

"Do you remember what it said?"

"Damn Judge," Cleve interrupted. "Get to the point."

"Alright then. Bebe read Buck's Will and refresh our memories of what it says."

"I'll do it. It's a round here somewhere. I know I had it this morning when I was cleaning the bathroom. Can't find it now." Mrs. Pithum tried to get up and look in the chair for the Will, but she was too tottery to stand.

"Don't fret none," said the Judge. "We'll write another one."

"No need for that," bellowed Mr. Speckman. "We all know what it says."

The lone hooded figure was totally ignored and remained motionless. It was like the black hood and robe were unoccupied by any living thing.

"Well then," said the Judge. "We'll go on about this little runt's indiscretion. Bebe get your typewriter off the floor and record these proceedings. We don't want a big high tone Atlanta lawyer coming down here saying we're doing something illegal when we ain't. It's time to hear testimony about this runt cheating on Buck's daughter. His one and only charming little southern belle. His beautiful daughter. His sugar baby," the Judge's voice vibrated in rhythm with his pulsating arthritic fingers as he screamed, **"LET'S HEAR IT NOW!!"** All at once, everyone turned toward the hooded figure and watched its black gloved hand creep towards its head. In a flash, the hand snatched the hood off in a flury of platinum blond hair.

"MY GOD!" I gasped. "IT'S LOVIE,"

"HE SCREWED ME!" she shouted pointing her black gloved hand at my head. In a spasm reflex, I fell to the floor and covered my head fearing she had a gun. They ignored my contorted body lying on the floor. And did nothing but moan and groan as she described my evil deed by making obscene gestures at her crotch. Then Lovie rolled her mascara-lined eyes toward heaven and whispered," Please forgive me Buck. He weren't near as good as you."

"WHAT!" I shouted shaking my fist in the Judge's face. "I've done nothing wrong. Yawl tried to set me up, but it didn't work. Lovie are you so drunk you've done lost your mind? I've had enough of this mess. I'm leaving. My inheritance is mine and there's nothing you can do about it."

CLANK! CLANK! CLANK!

The Judge's gavel banged on the metal bed railing. **"ORDER!** ORDER!," he barked. "You ain't gonna do nothing but hand over the deed to that land to me."

Before I had a chance to speak, I heard a faint voice ask,

"Do I still have to wear this hood? It's hot and it's messing up my hair."

"Lovie be quiet," answered the Judge. "Can't you see I'm talking to this boy?"

"I'm sorry. It's just too hot."

"Well then leave it off."

"Okay, I will."

The Judge removed a brass watch from his vest pocket; flipped its lid open and announced, "beginning now 9:27 p.m. the 8th day of November, 1976 it's my official duty to inform you that you've violated Mr. Mathas' Will." Two times the Judge tried to arise from his

Lazy Boy Recliner and two times he failed. On the third try, he was assisted by Rev. Boswell who was able to lift him to his feet. Ignoring his predicament, the Judge went on talking like nothing happened,

"I'm embarrassed to say the violation has come in the worst possible way. All Buck wanted in exchange for his daughter's virginity was your fidelity. He'd been willing to give you all his land if you'd been loyal to his daughter. His loving sugar baby Puddin. Lovie's testimony has shown us you're not worthy of either her virginity or his land." The Judge had now gotten to his feet and been able to speak with greater volume. "It's a great honor to stand before Buck's death bed this day and tell his spirit we're gonna enforce his Will and gut you like a hog and skin you like a skunk. From this day forward, your inheritance goes to me. And further more, if you're ever caught on Buck's land again you'll be arrested for trespassing."

CLANK! CLANK! CLANK!

The Judge banged the gavel on the metal bed railing again and said, "Sheriff Tate please remove this runt, this disgraceful piece of white trash from my sight and from the sight of these fine upstanding Haynesville citizens who've gathered here for this most blessed occasion."

Sheriff Tate, a sneer on his face, marched over to where I was lying on the floor and grabbed my arm.

"Don't touch me. Get out of my way," I said pushing him aside as I got up and stormed out of the room. The 'TOXIC WASTE' sign crashed to the floor with a glass breaking crunch as the door slammed shut behind me. That was my last meeting with those cold blooded killers.

I returned to Jonesboro after that meeting and never said a word to Puddin about it. All she wanted was to drive back to Haynesville and settle her mother's personal business with Judge Stoneridge which I now know involves that deadly church committee. So I knew when we left Jonesboro this morning this was going to be an unpleasant trip.

Chapter 16

The Trip Ends

A huge yellow ball, the sun, has caught the dusk and now runs to catch the darkness. Our trip is about to end as we continue west on the Peach Blossom Trail a two lane road running towards the setting sun. I tilt the sun visor down to shield its brightness from my eyes. Five more miles and our trip will end beside Vivian's grave. Five miles a distance that has isolated Haynesville from I-75 and the world.

I watch Puddin look into her sun visor's mirror and stroke her auburn hair with a comb and her eyebrows with her finger tips. We pass ranks of pecan trees marching by the roadside like soldiers on parade. Their leafless limbs piercing the fading gray winter sky.

"I've always admired these pecan trees along the Skipper's place," I tell her.

"Uh huh," she says, putting on lipstick.

I can't imagine why she's primping. All we're going to see is her dead mother Vivian.

The Haynesville water tower is off in the distance and the tall pecan trees soon give way to squatty peach trees. Next we're greeted by Haynesville's 'WELCOME' sign.

We pass the Hughes Motel's burned out remains. It had deteriorated over the past eight years and finally disappeared in a roaring flaming inferno. I'll always remember that motel because we had our wedding reception there.. A banquet table held a sumptuous dinner. China and silver sparkled in the candle light and laughter echoed off the pale yellow dining room walls. The motel's pool was freshly painted a marine blue and its crystal clear water shimmered in the summer's sun.. Now weeds cover the grounds where lush St. Augustine grass used to grow. Dead leaves fill the pool and its walls are riddled with cracks and crusted mold.

We turn off The Peach Blossom Trail onto Wayside St. where the town's one and only stoplight hangs over the intersection and where colorful signs used to direct snowbirds to motels, restaurants and gift shops. There are no cars with out of state license plates crowding the gas stations anymore and The Mathas Bros. Warehouse is empty. Its seeds and fertilizer smells a thing of the past. No railroad boxcars wait at its loading dock. All that is left are the memories of a by-gone era that will never return.

Going down Wayside St. we pass by Puddin's family home and The Haynesville Baptist Church. The remains of the Baptismal pool are all that had escaped the fire and lies naked amongst the charred timbers. A sign decorated with golden angels blowing long trumpets stands in the church yard heralding the words: SIGHT OF

THE NEW HAYNESVILLE BAPTIST CHURCH. Puddin notices how I cringe at its sight and proudly announces.

"Cleve's gonna rebuild the church right away. He's gonna make it bigger than it was. He's even gonna place a brass plate on the wall behind the Baptismal pool dedicating it: In loving memory of Mrs. Vivian Mathas. I know Mother would like that."

Next we turn onto the road leading to the cemetery and pass by a lot filled with wrecked cars. It's the place where Merietta's bloody car was parked and where the funeral procession paused to honor her sacrifice. We follow a small sandy road through wrought iron gates and under an archway supported by fluted marble post into the peach orchard. Its a beautiful place. Cleve's green houses have provided fresh flowers for each grave. It's the peach orchard Cleve had inherited from his daddy. But unlike his daddy, who grew peaches there all his life, Cleve had become a funeral director and began selling small pieces of land between the peach trees as cemetery plots. Eventually, he sold enough plots to renovate the old antebellum mansion in town and turned it into his funeral home. Unfortunately, there existed one major problem. His daddy's will stated the orchard was Cleve's as long as he grew peaches in it. Otherwise the orchard would go to his sister who lived in Thomasville. Cleve solved this problem by growing peaches and burying people in the orchard at the same time. Going to rest amongst the peach trees, the Haynesville folks loved so well, suited them just fine. To keep the pickers from getting spooked as they worked in the orchards, no tombstones were used to mark the grave sites. It was also important that no one knew the peaches being shipped throughout the U.S. and Canada were being grown in a graveyard.

When his sister died, Cleve turned the peach orchard into a real cemetery without fear of violating his daddy's will and it's now covered with tombstones. But there was one big problem. Cleve had recorded the names of those buried in the orchard over the years, but had failed to record the precise locations of their burial sights. Now it was anybody's guess where to place the tombstones. This resulted in tombstones being scattered willy-nilly throughout the cemetery. Tombstones are now so thick and out of line it's hard to drive to a grave site without hitting one. Weaving through the peach trees and tombstones like a crawling snake we finally stop in front of Mr. Mathas' mama and daddy's tombstones. Vivian lies on our left. A tall marble spire marks her grave. It cast a long thin shadow across the car's hood as the sun sets low on the horizon. It'll be dark soon. A knee high spear pointed wrought iron fence surrounds a grassy plot on our right. It's empty. According to Vivian's Will, Mr. Mathas' body is to be exhumed from the backyard of their home and placed in this empty plot. There he will spend eternity together with his mama and daddy and Vivian in the peach orchard. A bushel basket full of peaches is to be sprinkled over his grave each harvest to honor the words carved on his headstone: "HERE LIES THE PEACH KING of ORCHARD COUNTY".

"We're here at last," I sighed knowing I had done what Puddin wanted. Get to her mother's grave by dark. Expecting her thanks I turn to see her expressionless face in the strange glow of fading sunlight reflecting off the surrounding marble monuments. She neither stirs nor speaks. I hear the faint murmur from a car engine coming from behind us.. It's getting louder and louder as it comes closer and closer. I look in the rear view mirror and see a car's chrome grill and bumper. The hum from the car's engine stops. I turn to look out the back window and see a man in a broad brimmed hat getting out of the car. NO! It's Sheriff Tate with a shotgun under his arm. Frantically, I turn to Puddin my eyes pleading for help.

"I'm sorry it has to be this way," she says opening the door and with one last grunt steps out of the car and starts walking toward Sheriff Tate. My hands shaking, I race to start the engine, but I'm surrounded by tombstones. Vivian's is on my left side, Mr. Mathas' mother and fathers are in front of me and Mr. Mathas' iron fence surrounding his future burial site is on my right side. With Sheriff Tate's car behind me, I am completely surrounded and cannot move the car. I have no escape. In a panic, I lunge out the car door and land face down on a grass covered grave. I scurry to take cover behind its marble spire when I hear a loud blast from Sheriff Tate's shotgun. Pellets hiss by my head and hit the base of the marble spire blasting off the words:

HERE LIES MRS. VIVIAN MATHAS
FAITHFUL WIFE to BUCK MATHAS Jr.
1924 - 1976

Instantly I see them disappear in a cloud of marble dust which blinds me. Blind or not, I've gotta run if I'm going to survive another shotgun blast. Crouching behind one tombstone after the other, I run through the cemetery as fast as I can. I know the peach trees are thick only fifty yards away. I wipe the dust from my eyes. It's now dark. All I can see is the shadowed outlines of the peach trees. Make it there and I might be safe. I'm running fast as I can toward the trees when the ground crumbles under my feet causing me to stumble into a hole. It's dark and deep. I lie motionless face down in the dirt listening for the sound of twigs cracking under Sheriff Tate's boots. I hear nothing. The silence comforts me. No frogs croaking. No crickets chirping. It's winter and winter, the quietist of all seasons, makes no noise. Slowly, without a sound I turn over on my back and look up at the hole's rectangular opening silhouetted against the night's sky. MY GOD! I'm in a freshly dug grave. I've gotta get out of here. My feet digging and fingers scratching the dirt wall I lift my head out of the grave's opening enough to see a light flickering in the distance. I hear voices.

"Over here," I hear Sheriff Tate say. "I wanna show you where I'll bury him."

"You've already dug his grave?" Puddin asked.

"Oh yeah, I had it dug this morning as soon as you told me yawl were coming. Look it's by Fussel's grave. He'll like that," he says laughing.

Sheriff Tate's flashlight suddenly finds its mark and shines in my eyes. Blinded by the light, I can't see his face. All I see are the toes of his cowboy boots poking over the grave's dirt edge.

"Well lookie here," he says lowering the shotgun barrel toward my head.

Then I see Puddin's chubby knees floundering over the dirt trying to move her massive weight closer to the grave opening.

"What is it?" she asked, what's down there?"

It's Poon. Let me kill him,"

"No, no don't shoot HIM!"

"Why not?"

"It's gotta look like the others. An accident. Not murder. It's gotta look like he stumbled into this open grave and the dirt caved in on him."

"Damn Puddin, you're gonna be just like your mother."

"Get on your knees," she orders, "help me shove this dirt down on him."

"Bury him alive. I like it. Hell Puddin, you're gonna be better than your mother ever was."

Loose dirt begins falling all over me. My face, mouth, shoulders and feet are getting covered by loose dirt. I claw the wall with my fingers and feet trying to get out of the grave, but it's no use. With the dirt caving in all around me, there's nothing to grab on to.

"KEEP PUSHING! KEEP PUSHING!" Puddin shouts over and over again.

Dust fills my lungs muffling my screams for help. Covered by more and more dirt, my feet get heavier and heavier until I can no longer lift them in my attempts to climb up the walls. Dirt fills around my knees as they shove more and more dirt into the grave. It's the same dirt covering Grandma Mathas, Fussel, George, Merietta, Leafy, Mr. Mathas and Vivian's coffins and now I'm going to be buried in it too.

"Keep going," urges Puddin, "it's almost done."

Dirt covers my chest. I can hardly breathe. I gasp for air. My arms flailing to keep the dirt off me. But it's no use. I'm getting too weak to go on.

"DIE! DIE!" Puddin shouts. "I told you I'll never let Haynesville be another Pennyfield. Nothing's gonna stop me. Not even you."

"HOLD ON THERE! WHAT'S GOING ON HERE?!" I hear a loud voice come from somewhere in the distance. Choking on the dirt, I'm about to pass out when I hear,

"STOP OR I'LL SHOOT!"

The dirt stops falling on me and I lie lifeless looking up at the sky. Through the dust I see blurred flashlight beams dancing in unison over the grave's opening. Georgia State Troopers, bathed in the light's glow filtering through the dust, peer down at me through the grave's opening. Puddin and Sheriff Tate are still on their knees. No longer are their hands pushing dirt down on me. Two State Troopers jump into the grave and begin digging me out of the dirt.

"Call an ambulance," I hear one say.

Little by little they remove the dirt from my body and pull me from the grave still choking from the dust in my lungs. I sit on the dirt mound beside the grave choking from the dust and gasping for air as I try to explain. "I'm okay. I'm okay. Don't need an ambulance. The only ambulance here is Cleve's hearse and that's the last place I wanna be."

"Dr. Rutherford are you hurt?" I hear a familiar voice ask. It's Flavel's voice.

"I'm alright," I answer. "What are you doing here?"

"Charlie's done it. He convinced Mr. Ball that you were in danger of being killed and he got the State Troopers to come down here and check things out. Before yawl left this morning, I remembered Puddin saying the other day she wanted me to feed the dog while yawl were going to Haynesville. She also said she wanted to see her mother's grave. We couldn't find you anywhere else so we came here."

Then Charlie comes rushing over to where I'm sitting and puts his hand on my shoulder. We've done it by-golly. We've done it.

All these Georgia State Troopers just witnessed them trying to kill you. Bury you alive. That's the proof we needed to put all those cut throats away for good." Charlie's bulls eye target like eyes are open wide as fruit jar lids and he's talking real fast. Mr. Ball is here too, but he didn't wanna walk around in this cemetery at night. So, he stayed in the car. Charlie stood up on the mound of dirt from the freshly dug grave beside me and kept on talking. He was waving his arms in the air and talking louder and faster as he spoke. "On our trip down here, Mr. Ball said he wants me to be The Charity Life Insurance Co. lawyer and prosecute all of them for fraud. I'm sure I'll be in on the murder trial too. It'll be a big trial. I just know it. I'll be a big Atlanta lawyer. Might even be world famous. Flash lights swirling around the grave site shine on him for a few seconds. And as usual he looks like a Wall Street Charlie in his gray and blue pin-striped suit divided in the middle by a red and yellow striped neck tie. But his shiny black Italian loafers look out of place standing in the dirt. He leans down and puts his hand on my shoulder again and says, "Don't worry about Flavel. He's been so helpful to everybody I'm sure I can get him off scott free. Yawl can go off riding that yellow school bus into the sunset like conquering heroes."

I turned around to see the troopers lift Puddin and Sheriff Tate up off the dirt and walk away. As I watch her feet clumsily trample the dirt in an effort to keep her balance, I couldn't help but feel sorry for her. For she has lost her dream of saving Haynesville. The place where her daddy, The Peach King of Orchard County, once ruled with his Queen Vivian by his side while I had gotten my dream --- **THE LAND**.

The End

And the letter that was in the mailbox the morning our trip began. I finally opened it a month later. It was from Flavel warning me Sheriff Tate was going to kill me when I returned to Haynesville. I often wonder what a difference it might have made if I had opened it that morning.

About the Author

Dr. Jim Gerlock graduated from The Medical College of Georgia and completed a Radiology Residency at Tripler Army Medical Center, Walter Reed Army Hospitals. He received the Bronze Star Medal for his Vietnam service. After leaving the US Army Medical Corp. as a Colonel, he did a neurovascular and peripheral vascular angiographic fellowship at Baylor College of Medicine Houston, Texas.

He entered academic medicine and became Associate Professor of Radiology at Vanderbilt University Medical School and Director of the Interventional Radiology Dept. and Professor of Radiology at LSU. He has co-authored and drawn medical illustrations for some of his numerous published scientific articles and the following medical text books: Essentials of Diagnostic and Interventional Angiographic Techniques; Applications of Noninvasive Vascular Techniques; The Cervical Spine in Trauma; Clinical and Radiographic Interpretation of Facial Fractures; Emergency Radiology of the Shoulder, Arm and Hand.

His 3x4' oil on canvas painting "Elephants of The African Planes" was on exhibit at the National Institutes of Health for several years.

He is retired and lives in the beautiful city of Fort Myers Beach, Florida where he created the cartoon bird character Henry Heron and authored the book The Best of Henry Heron Cartoons. His cartoons have appeared in numerous Southwest Florida newspapers over a span of fourteen years.

Made in the USA
Columbia, SC
29 October 2017